Christmas with the Earl

A CLEAN REGENCY ROMANCE

DAISY LANDISH

BEACHES AND TRAILS
PUBLISHING

CHAPTER 1

A Proposal of Comfort

"Lord Ashford has inquired after you specifically." Lady Eleanor Winthrop read the words aloud from her aunt's letter, her voice dripping with the same disdain she might reserve for a particularly unappetizing dish. "Such a distinguished gentleman, and his estate in Derbyshire is said to be magnificent."

She set the cream-colored paper down with deliberate care, though her fingers itched to crumple it into oblivion. The morning light through the tall windows struck her as offensively cheerful, illuminating the stark reality of her aunt's latest matrimonial scheming.

"Magnificent estate," Nell muttered, rising from her writing desk to pace the length of the morning room. "As if the size of a man's holdings could fill the void in one's heart."

The miniature portrait at her throat caught the light as she moved—Isabella's face, forever young and radiant, forever frozen at nineteen with her whole life stretching ahead of her. Nell's fingers found the locket instinctively, a gesture that had become as natural as breathing in the eight months since her sister's death.

Eight months since Isabella had died, bringing the heir into the world—an heir who had followed his mother into eternal silence within hours of his birth. Eight months since Nell had worn anything but the deepest mourning, had danced, had laughed, had cared about any gentleman's prospects, magnificent or otherwise.

The truth that lurked beneath her grief was far more troubling than mere sorrow. It was the growing certainty that she would never measure up to Isabella's memory—not in beauty, not in charm, and certainly not in the effortless way her sister had captured hearts and brightened rooms simply by existing. How could Nell possibly meet Society's expectations when she felt like a pale shadow of the sister everyone had adored?

"Still refusing to be reasonable, I see."

Nell turned to find her mother in the doorway, elegant as always in dove-gray silk, her expression that familiar mixture of maternal concern and aristocratic exasperation.

"Good morning, Mama." Nell attempted a smile, smoothing her black silk skirts. "I was merely considering Aunt Margaret's latest correspondence."

Lady Fairfield glided into the room with the practiced grace of a woman who had successfully navigated three daughters through their Seasons. Two triumphantly, one with increasing frustration.

"Darling girl," she began, settling into the rose-colored chair near the fireplace, "surely you cannot mean to remain in mourning indefinitely. Society has begun to whisper, and your father grows concerned about your prospects."

The word 'prospects' hung in the air like smoke. Nell moved

to the window, watching the first lazy snowflakes of winter drift past the glass.

"What prospects could I possibly have that would honor Isabella's memory?" The question escaped before Nell could contain it, revealing more of her inner turmoil than she'd intended. "She was everything beautiful and gracious about our family. I am merely..."

"You are merely allowing grief to cloud your judgment," Lady Fairfield said firmly, rising to join her daughter at the window. "Isabella was indeed a treasure, but she would be horrified to know you're burying yourself alongside her memory."

Nell's laugh held no humor. "Would she? Sometimes I think the kindest thing I could do is withdraw entirely, spare Society the disappointment of comparing us."

"Eleanor Winthrop." Her mother's voice carried the authority of generations of well-bred women who had weathered their own storms. "I will not permit such morbid nonsense. You are not your sister, nor should you attempt to be. You have your own gifts, your own worth."

Before Nell could respond, inspiration struck with the sudden clarity of winter lightning.

"Lady Greystowe," she said, turning from the window with the first genuine animation she'd felt in weeks. "She wrote last month, didn't she? Mentioned how quiet Greystowe Hall has become since... well, since the tragedy."

Lady Fairfield's brow furrowed. "Yes, the poor dear. Losing both her son and daughter-in-law within hours of each other, and now with all the uncertainty about the estate's future. I believe she mentioned some correspondence with distant relations—something about the new heir finally taking an interest in his inheritance."

"She invited me to visit whenever I wished." Nell's words came faster now, the plan crystallizing in her mind. "To spend time with someone who loved Isabella as I did, who understands the weight of such loss."

"Yorkshire? In December?" Her mother's tone suggested Nell had proposed a journey to the Arctic. "My dear, it will be frightfully cold, and the roads treacherous. Besides, you'll know no one save the Dowager Countess herself."

"Precisely." Nell returned to her writing desk, already mentally composing her letter of acceptance. "No balls requiring my attendance, no suitors to deflect, no well-meaning relatives attempting to thrust eligible gentlemen into my path every time I venture from the house."

She pulled out a fresh sheet of paper, her movements decisive for the first time in months. "Just quiet companionship with someone who won't expect me to sparkle or charm or pretend that Isabella's absence hasn't carved a hole in the very fabric of existence."

Lady Fairfield was quiet for a long moment, studying her daughter's profile as Nell began to write. "You truly believe this will provide the solace you seek?"

"I believe," Nell said carefully, pausing in her writing, "that I need time away from London's expectations. Time to remember who I am when I'm not being constantly reminded of who I'm not." She looked up, meeting her mother's concerned gaze. "Lady Greystowe understands grief in a way that Lord Ashford's magnificent estate simply cannot address."

The silence stretched between them, filled only with the soft scratch of Nell's pen across the paper and the gentle patter of snow against the windows.

"Very well,' Lady Fairfield said finally, her voice gentler than before. "But you must give me your word on something."

Nell set down her pen. "Anything."

"Promise me you'll attempt to heal while you're there, not merely hide. Isabella would want you to find your way back to joy, not entomb yourself in perpetual mourning." Her mother's eyes misted slightly. "She loved you dearly, you know. Often spoke of how much she admired your spirit, your independence of thought."

The words hit Nell like a physical blow, so unexpected were they. Isabella had admired her? It seemed impossible, yet her mother's sincerity was unmistakable.

"I promise to try, Mama," Nell managed, her voice thick with emotion. "I cannot guarantee success, but I promise to make the attempt."

Lady Fairfield smiled, the first genuine expression of hope Nell had seen from her in months. "Then write your letter, my dear. Perhaps the Yorkshire air will indeed prove beneficial."

Three days later, despite her father's concerns about the weather and her maid's dire predictions about the state of northern roads in winter, Nell found herself seated in the family carriage as it wound through the gates of Greystowe Hall. Snow had begun falling in earnest during the final miles of their journey, transforming the ancient landscape into something from a fairy tale.

The estate stretched before her in winter splendor—rolling hills dusted white, venerable oaks standing sentinel along the drive, and finally, the great house itself rising from the snowy landscape with quiet authority. Greystowe Hall commanded its surroundings through sheer presence rather than ostentation, its weathered stone walls speaking of centuries of Christmases past, its windows glowing against the gathering dusk.

As the carriage rolled to a stop before the massive oak doors, they opened as if by magic, revealing a figure that made Nell's heart clench with bittersweet recognition. Lady Greystowe emerged, her silver hair perfectly arranged beneath a black lace cap, her mourning dress elegant in its simplicity. But it was her smile— warm, genuine, and touched with the same melancholy Nell carried—that brought tears to her eyes.

"My dearest girl," Lady Greystowe called as Nell descended from the carriage, her voice carrying both the crisp authority of nobility and genuine maternal affection. "How very good of you to make such a journey in this weather."

"Thank you for receiving me," Nell replied, accepting the older woman's embrace. The familiar scent of lavender and rosewater that had always surrounded Isabella's mother-in-law brought a fresh wave of memories—not painful ones, surprisingly, but warm recollections of family gatherings and shared laughter.

"Nonsense. You've done me the favor." Lady Greystowe linked their arms with practiced ease, guiding Nell toward the entrance. "This old house has been far too quiet these past months. I find I've grown quite weary of my own company and Mrs. Hartwell's well-meaning but repetitive observations about the weather."

As they crossed the threshold into the great hall, Nell felt some invisible weight begin to lift from her shoulders. The space was vast without being intimidating, warmed by an enormous fire crackling in the stone hearth and decorated with fresh evergreen boughs that filled the air with the crisp scent of winter holidays. Candles flickered in iron sconces along the walls, casting dancing shadows that seemed to welcome rather than threaten.

"It's beautiful," Nell said, meaning every word. The hall managed to be both grand and inviting—no small feat in a space that could easily have felt cold and forbidding.

"Isabella always said Christmas here felt like stepping into a storybook," Lady Greystowe replied, her voice catching slightly. "She had such elaborate plans for last year's celebration..." The older woman straightened her shoulders with visible effort. "But we mustn't dwell overmuch on what cannot be changed. Come, let's see you settled properly."

As they climbed the grand staircase, their footsteps echoing softly, Lady Greystowe continued her gentle chatter. "I've had Cook prepare a light supper for this evening, nothing too elaborate. The staff has been somewhat reduced since the changes, but Mrs. Hartwell runs the household with admirable efficiency."

"I'm hardly accustomed to grand ceremony," Nell assured her. "Simple comfort suits me perfectly."

They paused before a door painted the soft blue of a summer sky. "I hoped you might feel that way," Lady Greystowe said, opening the door to reveal a charming chamber with rose-pink hangings and a cheerful fire already dancing in the grate. "Isabella always said you possessed a refreshing lack of pretension."

As Nell stepped into the room, the scent of burning applewood and the sight of fresh linens turned down invitingly struck her with unexpected force. For the first time in eight months, she felt truly welcomed, not merely tolerated or pitied, but genuinely wanted. The sensation was so foreign she had to steady herself against the doorframe.

"Are you quite well, my dear?" Lady Greystowe asked with concern.

"Yes," Nell managed, her voice thick with gratitude. "Just... overwhelmed by your kindness."

As her hostess smiled and left her to settle, Nell moved to the window where snow continued to fall, blanketing Greystowe Hall in pristine silence and gradually sealing them away from the rest of the world. For the first time since Isabella's death, she thought that perhaps isolation might be exactly what her wounded heart required.

She had no way of knowing that her peaceful retreat was about to be thoroughly disrupted by the unexpected arrival of a man who desired solitude just as desperately as she did—and would prove far less willing to share it gracefully.

CHAPTER 2

Greystowe Hall

Nell woke to the soft patter of snow against her window and the distant sound of church bells from the village below. For a moment, she lay still in the unfamiliar bed, wrapped in the warmth of down quilts and the peculiar peace that comes from being somewhere no one expects anything of you.

The Blue Room was even lovelier in daylight than it had been by candlelight. Morning sun filtered through frost-etched windows, casting delicate patterns across the rose-pink hangings and polished wood floors. Someone, Mrs. Hartwell, she presumed, had already been in to stoke the fire and leave a basin of steaming water on the washstand.

Nell rose and moved to the window, pushing aside the heavy curtains to look out over the winter landscape. The view took her breath away. Snow had fallen steadily through the night, transforming the gardens into a pristine wonderland. Ancient yews stood like sentinels draped in white, and the bare branches of what must be magnificent roses in summer created intricate lacework against the pale sky.

Beyond the formal gardens, she could see the dark line of a forest and, in the distance, smoke rising from the chimneys of what appeared to be a small village. The entire scene looked like something from one of the fairy tales Isabella used to read aloud during their childhood—beautiful, peaceful, and utterly removed from the complexities of London life.

A soft knock at the door interrupted her reverie. "Come in," she called, expecting Mrs. Hartwell or perhaps a maid.

Instead, Lady Greystowe entered, already dressed for the day in an elegant morning gown of deep plum wool. Her silver hair was arranged in a simple but becoming style, and her eyes held a brightness that spoke of genuine pleasure.

"Good morning, my dear. I hope you slept well?" Lady Greystowe moved to stand beside Nell at the window, following her gaze out over the snowy landscape. "Rather different from London, isn't it?"

"It's magnificent," Nell said. "I don't think I've ever seen anything so peaceful."

"Isabella said the same thing when she first came here as a bride." Lady Greystowe's voice held only warmth now, the sharp edge of grief softened by happy memories. "She spent hours at this very window, planning improvements to the gardens. She had such ambitious ideas—a rose walk, an herb garden near the kitchens, even a small maze using the old boxwood hedges."

"Did she... were any of them completed?" Nell asked carefully.

"Oh yes, several. The rose walk is quite lovely in summer, though you can barely make it out under all this snow. And her herb garden has provided the kitchen with fresh seasonings for two years running now." Lady Greystowe smiled. "She would be pleased to know her ideas took root, quite literally."

They stood in comfortable silence for a few moments, watching fat snowflakes drift past the window, the shared memory of Isabella settling between them like the falling snow—gentle, persistent, impossible to ignore.

At length, Lady Greystowe stirred, her expression softening into something more resolute. "It does no good to dwell only in the past," she said, as much to herself as to Nell. "Come—perhaps a tour of the house might lift our spirits."

She gestured for them to follow. "It's been so long since we've had proper guests, and I confess I'm rather eager to show off Isabella's improvements. She had an excellent eye for both beauty and practicality."

"I would love that," Nell said, meaning it. The prospect of learning more about how her sister had made her mark on this ancient place held unexpected appeal.

"Splendid. Mrs. Hartwell has prepared a breakfast tray for the morning room—nothing elaborate, but Cook does make the most delightful scones. Shall we say in half an hour?"

After Lady Greystowe departed, Nell dressed carefully in one of her simpler morning gowns—black wool trimmed with jet buttons, appropriate for her mourning but not so severe as to cast a pall over the day. She arranged her dark hair in a neat chignon and pinned Isabella's locket at her throat, as had become her custom.

The morning room proved to be a charming space overlooking what Lady Greystowe informed her were the kitchen gardens. Windows on two sides filled the room with light, and a small fire crackled cheerfully in the grate. The promised breakfast was indeed delightful—warm scones with butter and jam, strong tea, and thin slices of ham that Cook had somehow managed to cure to perfection despite the reduced household.

"The kitchens are Mrs. Hartwell's domain," Lady Greystowe explained as they ate. "She's been here since before my late son was born, and I don't believe there's anything related to the running of this house that she doesn't know. The woman is worth her weight in gold, particularly now that we're operating with a skeleton staff."

"Have many of the servants found other positions?" Nell asked, then immediately regretted the question as potentially too personal.

But Lady Greystowe seemed happy to discuss the practical matters. "Some, yes. When it became clear that the new earl might not... Well, that the future of the estate was uncertain, I encouraged several of the younger staff to seek employment elsewhere. Better to find good positions while they can than wait and risk being turned off without references." She took a delicate sip of tea. "Though I must say, those who chose to remain have been utterly loyal. I couldn't ask for better support during such a difficult time."

After breakfast, Lady Greystowe proved to be an excellent guide through the sprawling house. They began in the formal drawing room, where family portraits gazed down from gilded frames, and silk-covered furniture spoke of generations of refined living. Nell found herself searching the faces in the paintings for any resemblance to Isabella, but the Greystowe features seemed to run to dark hair and strong jawlines rather than her sister's fair beauty.

"The library is my particular pride," Lady Greystowe said as they entered a magnificent room lined floor to ceiling with leather-bound volumes. Tall windows provided excellent reading light, and several comfortable chairs were positioned near the fireplace. "My late husband was quite the scholar, and his father before him. Some of these books date back two centuries."

Nell ran her fingers along the spines, marveling at the collection. "Isabella must have loved this room."

"Indeed, she did. She spent many evenings here, particularly during..." Lady Greystowe paused, seeming to choose her words carefully. "During the later months, when she was not feeling quite herself. She found great comfort in poetry, I believe."

They continued through the house—the formal dining room with its massive table that could seat twenty, the conservatory where exotic plants somehow thrived despite the winter cold, and several guest chambers that rivaled Nell's own in comfort and elegance. Each room told a story of family history and careful maintenance, even with the reduced staff.

"The estate has been in the Greystowe family for over three hundred years," Lady Greystowe explained as they paused in what had clearly been the master's study. "Each generation has added its own touches while respecting what came before. It's quite a legacy to inherit."

Something in her tone made Nell look at her more closely. "You speak as though you're not certain that legacy will continue."

Lady Greystowe moved to the window, gazing out at the snow-covered grounds with an expression that mingled love and worry. "The new earl is... shall we say, a practical man. A military man, with a soldier's view of sentiment versus necessity. I fear he may see Greystowe Hall as more of a burden than a blessing."

"Surely he wouldn't sell such a beautiful estate?"

"In truth, I do not know." Lady Greystowe's voice carried a weight of uncertainty that made Nell's heart ache for her. "We've had very little correspondence since he inherited. A few formal letters from his solicitors, notification that he was concluding his military service... but nothing to indicate his intentions regarding the estate or, indeed, his intentions to visit at all."

They were interrupted by the sound of the front door opening with considerable force, followed by voices in the great hall below. Lady Greystowe frowned, moving quickly toward the study door.

"That's odd. We're not expecting anyone, and in this weather..." She paused, listening to what sounded like Mrs. Hartwell's voice, unusually flustered, speaking to someone in urgent, low tones.

A man's voice replied—cultured, authoritative, and distinctly displeased about something. Nell couldn't make out the words, but the tone suggested someone accustomed to being obeyed without question.

Lady Greystowe's face went pale, then flushed with what appeared to be a mixture of surprise and dismay. "Oh dear. Oh my dear. I do believe..."

Heavy footsteps could be heard ascending the main staircase, accompanied by Mrs. Hartwell's continued protests about the propriety of arriving unannounced and the state of the roads and whether his lordship had taken proper care not to catch his death in such weather.

"Thomas," Lady Greystowe murmured, pressing a hand to her throat. "It must be Thomas."

Before Nell could ask who Thomas might be, the footsteps

reached the landing and approached the study. Lady Greystowe straightened her shoulders and moved toward the door, clearly preparing to greet whoever was about to enter.

The door opened without ceremony, and Nell found herself face to face with a tall man in a many-caped greatcoat still dusted with snow. Dark hair showed beneath a beaver hat that had seen better days, and keen gray eyes swept the room with the systematic thoroughness of someone conducting a military inspection.

Those gray eyes paused on Nell with unmistakable surprise before moving to Lady Greystowe with what could only be described as resignation.

"Aunt Margaret," the man said, removing his hat and offering a perfunctory bow. His voice held the clipped precision of someone accustomed to giving orders. "I hope you'll forgive the intrusion. The roads were worse than expected, and I thought it best to push through rather than risk being stranded at some coaching inn."

"Thomas.' Lady Greystowe moved forward, her hands extended in welcome despite the obvious shock of his unexpected arrival. "My dear boy, what a surprise. We had no word you were coming."

"No word seemed advisable," he replied curtly, allowing her to clasp his hands briefly before stepping back. "I prefer to see things as they actually are, rather than as they're prepared to be seen."

His gaze moved back to Nell, and his jaw tightened slightly. But for just a moment—so briefly she might have imagined it—something else flickered across his features. Recognition, perhaps, or confusion. As if he were seeing something he hadn't expected to find.

When he spoke again, his voice carried a distinct chill that seemed almost deliberately imposed.

"I was not aware we were entertaining houseguests."

The censure in his tone was unmistakable, and Nell felt her cheeks burn with embarrassment and rising indignation. Lady Greystowe, however, drew herself up with all the dignity of her rank.

"Lady Eleanor Winthrop is a most welcome guest," she said firmly. "The daughter of Viscount Fairfield, and Isabella's dear sister. She has kindly agreed to spend the Christmas season with me."

"Has she indeed?" Thomas—the new Earl of Greystowe, Nell realized with growing dismay—looked her up and down with the sort of assessment one might give a problem to solve. "How... convenient."

The word dripped with implications that made Nell's temper flare. She had come seeking peace, not to be treated like a fortune-hunting interloper by a man who hadn't even had the courtesy to announce his arrival.

"My lord," she said, dropping the best curtsy protocol demanded while managing to make it somehow seem like a challenge. "I do hope my presence won't inconvenience you unduly."

The smile that accompanied her words was perfectly polite and absolutely glacial.

Thomas studied her for a long moment, and Nell had the uncomfortable feeling he was seeing rather more than she intended to reveal. His expression shifted almost imperceptibly— the hard lines around his eyes softened for just an instant before he caught himself and resumed his stern demeanor.

When he finally spoke, his tone remained coolly formal, though something underneath suggested he was fighting to maintain that distance.

"Not at all, Lady Eleanor. I'm sure we shall manage to accommodate one another perfectly well."

Nell turned away before she could read more into the narrowing of his eyes, but not quickly enough to miss his quiet murmur as he passed his aunt.

"God help us if she's anything like her sister."

The words struck like cold water. Her spine stiffened. Whatever spark of grudging interest she'd felt moments ago shriveled beneath the weight of his condescension. So he thought her a pale imitation, then—perhaps just another decorative burden left behind by the dead.

The way he said it suggested he believed no such thing, yet there was an odd hesitation in his voice, as if he weren't entirely convinced of his own antagonism.

Lady Greystowe, clearly sensing the tension crackling between them, stepped smoothly into the breach. "Thomas, you must be exhausted after such a journey in this weather. Let me have Mrs. Hartwell prepare the Earl's chambers, and perhaps you'd care to join us for luncheon once you've had a chance to refresh yourself?"

"That would be acceptable," Thomas replied, his attention still fixed on Nell with an intensity that made her distinctly uncomfortable. "I trust we'll have ample opportunity to become better acquainted during my stay."

His tone softened almost imperceptibly on the last words, and for a moment, Nell wondered if she had misjudged his meaning entirely.

After he departed to see about his rooms, leaving his snow-dampened greatcoat draped over a chair and an uncomfortable silence in his wake, Lady Greystowe turned to Nell with an expression of sincere apology.

"My dear, I am so sorry. Thomas has always been rather... direct in his manner, but I fear military life has made him even more so. Please don't take his brusqueness to heart."

But there was something in Lady Greystowe's eyes—a calculating gleam that hadn't been there before, as though she were suddenly seeing possibilities she hadn't previously considered.

Nell managed a smile, though she could still feel the echo of those gray eyes studying her with such obvious suspicion—and something else she couldn't quite identify. "Of course not. It's his home, after all. I'm the intruder here."

"Nonsense," Lady Greystowe said firmly, though her tone had acquired a thoughtful quality. "You are my invited guest, and you are most welcome. Thomas will simply have to adjust his expectations accordingly."

But as they made their way back toward the morning room, Nell couldn't shake the feeling that adjusting expectations was going to prove far more complicated than Lady Greystowe anticipated. The Earl of Greystowe had looked at her like a threat to eliminate—yet something in those final moments suggested his antagonism might not be as straightforward as it appeared.

Either way, her peaceful retreat had just become significantly more complicated.

The snow continued to fall outside the windows, each flake adding to the growing barrier between Greystowe Hall and the outside world. They were well and truly snowed in now, Nell realized, trapped together whether they liked it or not.

Somehow, she suspected the Earl liked it even less than she did.

But perhaps, just perhaps, his protests weren't quite as convincing as he wanted them to be.

CHAPTER 3

The Unexpected Heir

Thomas Greystowe stood before the mirror in what had once been his cousin's dressing room, methodically removing the travel stains from his appearance while his mind worked through the unexpected complications that had greeted his arrival at Greystowe Hall.

He had come here with a simple purpose: to assess the estate's condition, settle its affairs, and determine whether sentiment or practicality should guide his decisions about its future. What he had not anticipated was finding his aunt entertaining a house-guest, particularly one who looked at him with such clear, intelligent eyes and spoke with such pointed politeness.

Lady Eleanor Winthrop. Isabella's sister.

Thomas paused, his hands stilling on the fresh cravat. He had met Isabella only once, at her wedding to his cousin, but the resemblance was unmistakable in the elegant line of Lady Eleanor's neck, the graceful way she held herself, even the stubborn tilt of her chin when challenged. Yet where Isabella had been all golden warmth and gentle charm, this sister possessed something altogether more formidable.

The way she had looked at him when he'd questioned her presence—as though he were an intruder in his own inherited home—had been both infuriating and oddly impressive. Most young ladies of his acquaintance would have stammered apologies or dissolved into tears under such scrutiny. Lady Eleanor had simply smiled that frost-edged smile and made it clear she found his manners wanting.

Which, if he were being honest, they probably were.

It stirred something he rarely acknowledged—an echo of the old ache he had buried beneath orders and battle reports. In quieter moments, when duty didn't press at his heels, he could still feel the hollow where simpler things used to live: affection, ease, the luxury of being understood without explanation. He had trained himself not to want those things. But looking at Lady Eleanor, with her sharp eyes and steady spine, he felt the ghost of wanting stir.

Thomas finished adjusting his cravat with more force than necessary. He had grown accustomed to military directness, to speaking plainly and expecting immediate comprehension. The subtle dance of social niceties had never been his strength, even before eight years of army life had further eroded his patience for drawing-room diplomacy.

But still. He might have been more civil.

The problem was that Lady Eleanor's presence complicated everything. He had hoped to spend these few days in quiet assessment, perhaps walking the estate boundaries, reviewing the account books, and having frank discussions with his aunt about the property's viability. Instead, he would be forced to make polite conversation and pretend an interest in whatever seasonal festivities his aunt had no doubt planned for her guest's entertainment.

He had not come here to indulge in sentiment, least of all directed toward his aunt's guest. And yet something about Lady Eleanor's defensive pride had stirred an unwelcome flicker of curiosity.

A sharp knock interrupted his brooding. "Come," he called, expecting his valet or perhaps Mrs. Hartwell with some domestic inquiry.

Instead, his aunt entered, having clearly taken time to compose herself since their earlier encounter. She wore the expression he remembered from childhood—the one that suggested he was about to receive instruction whether he wished it or not.

"Thomas," she began without preamble, "we must speak."

"Indeed, we must." Thomas turned from the mirror, gesturing to the chairs arranged near the window. "Please, sit. I apologize for arriving without notice, but I thought it best to see the estate's true condition rather than its holiday presentation."

Lady Greystowe settled herself with the regal bearing that came naturally to women of her generation. "And what, precisely, do you expect to find? Evidence that I've been running the place into the ground in your absence?"

The sharpness in her tone surprised him. His aunt had always been formidable, but this edge was new—or perhaps he simply hadn't been old enough to notice it before.

"Not at all," Thomas replied carefully. "But I needed to understand what I've inherited before making any decisions about its future."

"Ah." Lady Greystowe's expression grew thoughtful. "So you have not yet decided whether to keep Greystowe Hall."

It wasn't a question, and Thomas found himself oddly reluctant to confirm her suspicions. "I am... considering all options."

"I see. And Lady Eleanor's presence interferes with this consideration?"

"Her presence was unexpected," Thomas said, choosing his words with military precision. "I had hoped for privacy during my assessment."

"Privacy." Lady Greystowe repeated the word as though it left a bad taste. "Thomas, you have been absent from this family for eight years. You inherited an earldom, an estate, and responsibilities you never sought, and your response has been to conduct yourself like a property assessor rather than the head of a family."

The criticism stung because it held more than a grain of truth. "I am a soldier, Aunt Margaret. I understand duty and responsibility. But I also understand the difference between sentiment and practicality."

"Do you indeed?" Lady Greystowe rose and moved to the window, gazing out at the snow-covered grounds. "Tell me, Thomas, what do you see when you look at Greystowe Hall?"

Thomas joined her at the window, following her gaze across the winter landscape. "I see a large estate requiring significant investment to maintain properly. I see a house too grand for its current circumstances, a reduced staff, and agricultural lands that may or may not provide adequate income to support the whole."

"And that is all?"

The question hung between them, weighted with expectation. Thomas looked again, trying to see beyond the practical concerns that had dominated his thoughts since inheriting the title.

The snow had transformed the gardens into something almost magical. Ancient trees stood draped in white, their bare branches creating intricate patterns against the pale sky. In the distance, smoke rose from the village chimneys, and he could just make out figures moving along what must be the main street. It was beautiful, certainly, but beauty was a luxury he had learned not to trust.

"What would you have me see?" he asked finally.

"Three hundred years of family history. Generations of Greystowes who built something lasting, something meaningful. Your cousin's improvements, your great-grandfather's folly that became the most admired conservatory in the county." Lady Greystowe's voice softened. "The place where Isabella found happiness, however briefly."

At the mention of Isabella, Thomas felt an unexpected tightness in his chest. He had barely known his cousin's wife, but her death had affected him more than he'd anticipated. Perhaps because it had driven home the fragility of the happiness he'd never allowed himself to seek.

"I do not discount the history," he said quietly. "But history does not pay for roof repairs or servants' wages."

"No," Lady Greystowe agreed. "But it provides something money cannot buy—a sense of belonging, of purpose beyond mere survival." She turned to face him directly. "Tell me, Thomas, when did you last feel truly at home anywhere?"

The question caught him off guard. When had he last felt at home? In his tent on the Peninsula, surrounded by his men and united by common purpose? In his London lodgings, sparse and functional? The answer, he realized with some discomfort, was nowhere.

"That is neither here nor there," he said, deflecting. "My personal comfort is hardly the issue."

"Isn't it?" Lady Greystowe's smile held a hint of the mischief he remembered from his youth. "You know, Eleanor asked much the same question about belonging when we spoke this morning."

Thomas found himself unexpectedly curious about what else Lady Eleanor might have said, but he refused to give his aunt the satisfaction of asking.

"I should dress for luncheon," he said instead, moving toward his wardrobe. "I trust the meal will provide an opportunity to become better acquainted with your guest."

"Oh, I believe it will indeed," Lady Greystowe replied, and there was something in her tone that made Thomas pause in his selection of waistcoats.

"Aunt Margaret, you are not planning some sort of match-making scheme, are you?"

Lady Greystowe's expression was the picture of innocence. "My dear boy, Lady Eleanor is in mourning for her beloved sister. She has come here seeking peace and quiet companionship. The furthest thing from her mind would be an unsuitable attachment to a stranger."

The way she emphasized 'stranger' suggested Thomas's behavior had not escaped her notice or approval.

"Good," he said, though he wasn't entirely sure why the confirmation should provide such mixed feelings. "Because I have neither the time nor the inclination for drawing-room flirtations."

"Of course not," Lady Greystowe agreed placidly. "Though you might consider that even soldiers require allies, and Lady

Eleanor has already proven herself capable of defending her position when challenged."

With that cryptic comment, she departed, leaving Thomas to contemplate the implications of her words while he finished dressing.

When he finally made his way downstairs, he found the two ladies in the morning room, engaged in what appeared to be a spirited discussion about the proper way to preserve evergreen boughs for holiday decorations. Lady Eleanor was laughing at something his aunt had said, and the sound was unexpectedly musical— nothing like the cool, controlled voice she had used when speaking to him.

"Thomas," Lady Greystowe said as he appeared in the doorway, "perfect timing. Lady Eleanor has been telling me about the Christmas traditions at her family's estate. Apparently, they have quite elaborate celebrations."

"Indeed?" Thomas took the chair opposite Lady Eleanor, noting how her expression grew more guarded as he settled himself. "I'm afraid military Christmases tend toward the functional rather than the festive."

"How disappointing for you," Lady Eleanor replied, though her tone suggested she found his military Christmases entirely predictable rather than pitiable. "Though I suppose celebrating the season requires a certain appreciation for joy and tradition."

The subtle barb hit its mark, but Thomas found himself almost admiring her technique. "Quite so. I've found that survival tends to take precedence over sentiment in most circumstances."

"How fortunate, then, that you find yourself in circumstances where survival is assured and sentiment might be permitted."

Mrs. Hartwell's arrival with the luncheon service prevented

Thomas from formulating a response to that particular thrust. As they settled into their meal—an excellent soup, fresh bread, and what appeared to be the last of the autumn vegetables from the estate gardens—Lady Greystowe smoothly guided the conversation toward safer topics.

Try as he might to focus on his aunt's commentary about estate matters and village news, Thomas found his gaze returning to Lady Eleanor. Her poised manner as she navigated the conversation, the way her eyes lit with genuine interest when Lady Greystowe spoke of the tenants' Christmas traditions, the graceful movement of her hands as she gestured—all of it suggested a refinement born of genuine breeding rather than mere social training.

He was observing the delicate way she handled her spoon when she suddenly looked up, catching him in his study of her. For a moment, their gazes held, and Thomas felt an odd jolt of awareness pass between them. Lady Eleanor's cheeks colored faintly, but she didn't look away immediately. Instead, she tilted her head slightly, as if trying to puzzle out what she had seen in his expression.

Thomas cleared his throat and reached for his water glass, annoyed at himself for being caught staring like a green boy. What was it about her unguarded moments that made observation seem so effortless? When her defensive walls were lowered, as they were now in his aunt's gentle company, Lady Eleanor possessed a warmth that was entirely too appealing for his peace of mind.

"I was just telling Eleanor about the Boxing Day tradition in the village," Lady Greystowe said, and Thomas realized he had missed part of the conversation entirely. "Perhaps you might escort us when we deliver the gifts to the tenants?"

"If the weather permits," Thomas replied, though he was already calculating whether such an excursion would interfere with his planned inspection of the estate accounts.

"Oh, it will be tolerable enough by then," Lady Eleanor said with the confidence of someone accustomed to getting her way. "I'm told Yorkshire snow is far more cooperative than its reputation suggests."

"Told by whom?" Thomas asked, genuinely curious. "Have you visited the region before?"

"No, this is my first time so far north. But I have it on good authority from several sources." Lady Eleanor's smile held a hint of mischief that reminded him suddenly of his aunt. "Including Mrs. Hartwell, who assures me the roads will be clear enough for local travel within a day or two."

Thomas found himself wondering if Lady Eleanor was as eager to escape Greystowe Hall as he was to see her gone, or if she simply enjoyed being right about practical matters. Either way, the prospect of traveling through the countryside with both ladies in tow was beginning to seem less onerous than it had initially.

More troubling: he was beginning to look forward to it.

"Then we shall certainly consider it," he said, surprised by his own words.

Lady Greystowe's satisfied smile suggested she had orchestrated this entire exchange, though Thomas couldn't quite see how. As the meal concluded and they prepared to retire to the drawing room, he realized that his careful plans for a solitary assessment of his inheritance had been thoroughly disrupted.

The question was whether Lady Eleanor Winthrop represented an unwelcome complication, or an unexpected opportunity to see Greystowe Hall through different eyes entirely.

Either way, he suspected the next few days would prove far more interesting than he had anticipated.

And far more dangerous to the reserve he had cultivated so diligently over years of command.

CHAPTER 4

Snowbound

Nell woke the next morning to an ominous silence that spoke of weather far worse than the gentle snowfall of the previous day. When she pushed back the heavy curtains of the Blue Room, she gasped at what greeted her beyond the frost-etched glass.

Snow had fallen throughout the night with a vengeance that transformed the already pristine landscape into something almost otherworldly. The carefully tended gardens had disappeared entirely beneath drifts that reached nearly to the lower branches of the ancient yews. The drive was invisible, marked only by the tops of the stone posts that flanked the entrance gates. Even the forest beyond seemed muffled and distant, as though Greystowe Hall had been transported to some enchanted realm where time itself moved differently.

More concerning was the complete absence of any movement in the village beyond. No smoke rose from chimneys, no figures moved along what should have been the main street. It was as though the world beyond the estate had simply ceased to exist.

A soft knock interrupted her contemplation of their isolation. "Come in," she called, expecting Mrs. Hartwell with her morning chocolate.

Instead, Lady Greystowe entered, already dressed but wearing an expression of mingled concern and resignation that immediately put Nell on alert.

"Good morning, my dear. I'm afraid I bring rather dramatic news." Lady Greystowe moved to join Nell at the window, surveying the transformed landscape with the practiced eye of someone who had weathered many Yorkshire winters. "We are well and truly snowbound, it appears. Cook estimates we've received nearly three feet overnight, with drifts considerably higher in places."

"How long do such storms typically last?" Nell asked, though she suspected she already knew the answer from Lady Greystowe's expression.

"That depends entirely on when the wind dies down and whether we get more snow today. But I'm afraid we must prepare ourselves for several days of confinement at the very least." Lady Greystowe's tone grew apologetic. "I do hope this won't prove too tedious for you, my dear. I fear our entertainment options are rather limited under the circumstances."

Nell found herself oddly unconcerned by the prospect of extended isolation. Indeed, there was something rather liberating about being completely cut off from the expectations and obligations of the outside world. No letters could arrive demanding her attention to social engagements she had no desire to attend. No well-meaning relatives could suddenly appear with new schemes for her matrimonial future.

"I think I shall manage quite well," she said, meaning it. "Though I confess I'm rather curious how Lord Greystowe will react to having his assessment schedule disrupted so thoroughly."

Lady Greystowe's smile took on a decidedly mischievous quality. "Thomas has always prided himself on his ability to adapt to changing circumstances. Though I suspect being trapped indoors with two women and limited occupation will test even his military patience."

As if summoned by their discussion, the sound of heavy foot-steps in the corridor announced the Earl's approach. His knock was perfunctory—clearly a man accustomed to entering rooms without ceremony but making the gesture toward propriety.

"Aunt Margaret, I trust you've seen the conditions outside," Thomas said as he entered, still wearing his dressing gown and with his dark hair slightly disheveled. The informal attire made him appear younger, less intense, and Nell found herself noticing details she had missed the previous day—the breadth of his shoul-ders, the way his gray eyes seemed lighter in the morning sun, the small scar that ran along his left temple.

"Indeed, we have," Lady Greystowe replied. "Lady Eleanor and I were just discussing how we might best occupy ourselves during our enforced confinement."

Thomas's gaze moved to Nell, and she saw him take in her appearance with the same systematic thoroughness he had displayed the day before. Self-consciously, she realized she was still in her nightgown and wrapper, her dark hair hanging loose about her shoulders. Heat rose in her cheeks as she moved instinctively to put more distance between them.

"My apologies," Thomas said, his voice slightly rougher than usual. "I didn't realize... that is, I should have waited to be properly announced."

"Nonsense," Lady Greystowe said briskly, though Nell noticed the calculating gleam in her eyes. "We are quite beyond such formalities under the circumstances. Besides, Eleanor is perfectly decent, and we are all family here, are we not?"

The word 'family' seemed to hang in the air with unintended significance. Thomas cleared his throat and moved to the window, deliberately turning his back to afford Nell what privacy he could.

"The roads will be impassable for at least three days," he said, his tone returning to its usual crisp authority. "Possibly longer if we receive more snow today, which seems likely given the wind patterns."

"Then we shall simply have to make the best of it," Lady Greystowe declared with the sort of cheerful determination that suggested she was not entirely displeased by their predicament. "In fact, I believe this presents an excellent opportunity to begin our Christmas preparations in earnest."

Nell saw Thomas's shoulders tense at the word 'Christmas,' though his voice remained neutral. "I suppose idleness is preferable to futile attempts at travel in such conditions."

"Idleness?" Lady Greystowe's eyebrows rose in a manner that boded ill for Thomas's hopes of solitude. "My dear boy, there is nothing idle about preparing for Christmas. Eleanor and I were just discussing the decoration of the great hall, and there are gifts to be wrapped, menus to be planned, and any number of seasonal traditions that require attention."

"Of course," Thomas replied, and Nell detected a note of resignation that made her suspect he was beginning to realize exactly how his aunt intended to occupy their time. "I shall endeavor to assist wherever possible."

"Splendid. In that case, perhaps you could gather evergreen boughs from the conservatory and the protected areas near the house. Eleanor and I can hardly venture out in such weather, but a strong man with proper boots should manage quite well."

Thomas turned back toward them, and Nell caught a flash of something that might have been amusement in his expression. "You wish me to serve as your personal foraging expedition?"

"Unless you have more pressing engagements?" Lady Greystowe inquired with perfect innocence.

The brief silence that followed was filled with unspoken acknowledgment that Thomas's carefully planned assessment of the estate had been thoroughly derailed by Mother Nature herself.

"I believe my schedule has become remarkably flexible," he said finally. "Very well. I shall see about procuring sufficient greenery for whatever decorative schemes you have in mind."

"Excellent. Eleanor, perhaps you might assist Thomas in determining what sorts of boughs would be most suitable? You mentioned having experience with holiday decorations at your family's estate."

Nell felt a moment of panic at the prospect of being alone with the Earl, particularly while she was still in her nightclothes. But Lady Greystowe's expectant expression brooked no argument, and she could hardly confess to feeling unsettled by his presence without inviting questions she preferred not to answer.

"Certainly," she managed, though her voice sounded higher than usual. "Though I should dress first, naturally."

"Naturally," Thomas agreed, and she thought she detected a hint of relief in his tone. "Shall we say in an hour? That should provide sufficient time for us both to prepare for our expedition."

After he departed, Lady Greystowe turned to Nell with a smile that was far too satisfied for comfort.

"How fortunate that Thomas is so willing to help with our preparations," she said. "And how convenient that you have experience to guide him. I do believe this confinement may prove quite... educational for both of you."

Nell had the distinct impression that Lady Greystowe's definition of 'educational' encompassed far more than holiday decorating techniques.

An hour later, properly dressed in her warmest wool gown and with her hair neatly arranged, Nell met Thomas in the conservatory. The glass-walled space was surprisingly warm despite the frigid conditions outside, heated by some ingenious system of pipes that carried warmth from the main house. Exotic plants that should have been dormant in winter thrived in the controlled environment, creating an almost tropical oasis amidst the Yorkshire winter.

Thomas had clearly taken his foraging mission seriously. He wore sturdy boots, thick gloves, and a heavy coat that emphasized his military bearing. In his hands, he carried what appeared to be a small ax and several lengths of rope.

"I thought we might start with the hardy evergreens near the kitchen gardens," he said without preamble. "The snow has bent many of the branches low enough to reach safely, and Mrs. Hartwell assures me Cook won't mind sacrificing a few limbs for the cause of Christmas spirit."

"That sounds perfectly sensible," Nell replied, surprised by his thoroughness. She had expected him to approach the task with the grudging efficiency of a man fulfilling an unwelcome obligation. Instead, he seemed to have given considerable thought to the practical aspects of their mission.

They made their way carefully through the conservatory and out a side door that led to the protected areas behind the main house. The cold hit Nell like a physical blow, despite her warm clothing, and she gasped at the intensity of it.

"Perhaps you should remain inside," Thomas suggested, noting her reaction. "I can gather what we need and bring it to you for assessment."

"Absolutely not," Nell replied with more vehemence than she intended. "I'm hardly so delicate that I cannot tolerate a bit of fresh air."

Thomas studied her for a moment, and she thought she saw a hint of approval in his expression. "Very well. But stay close and tell me immediately if you become too cold."

As they worked their way through the snow-laden garden, selecting the best branches and discussing the merits of different types of evergreen boughs, Nell found herself enjoying the collaboration more than she had expected. Thomas approached the task with the same systematic thoroughness he seemed to bring to everything, but there was something almost playful in the way he tested branches for fullness and debated the aesthetic merits of pine versus fir.

The snow was deeper than anticipated in places, and more than once, Nell found herself struggling with the uneven terrain beneath the pristine surface. When she stumbled slightly over a hidden root, Thomas reached out instinctively, steadying her with a firm hand to her elbow. The contact was brief, but it left her unaccountably breathless, and she was grateful for the cold air that might explain the flush in her cheeks.

"Careful," he said, his voice gentler than usual. "The ground is more treacherous than it appears."

Nell drew back as soon as she was steady, brushing snow from her gloves with exaggerated focus. "Yes, well. I wouldn't want to be another liability."

Thomas blinked, his mouth opening as if to speak, then closing again. He turned back to the pine boughs with renewed intensity, the moment vanishing beneath a drift of silence too thick to wade through.

"Lady Greystowe once told me Isabella favored holly," he said at one point, carefully cutting a branch laden with bright red berries. "She claimed the contrast of the berries against the green was essential for proper Christmas spirit." It was the first time he had mentioned Isabella without prompting, and Nell felt a flutter of surprise at the casual way he spoke of her sister.

"She was right," Nell said softly. "Isabella had excellent taste in such matters. Our Christmas decorations at home were always magnificent when she was in charge of them."

Thomas paused in his cutting, glancing at her with an expression she couldn't quite read. "You must miss her terribly during the holidays."

The simple statement, offered without pity or excessive sympathy, somehow touched Nell more deeply than all the elaborate condolences she had received in London.

"I do," she admitted. "Last Christmas was... difficult. I couldn't bear the thought of celebrating anything when she was so recently gone."

"And this year?"

Nell considered the question as she watched Thomas carefully wrap the cut branches in the cloth they had brought to protect them during transport. "This year feels different somehow. Perhaps it's being here, where she was happy. Or perhaps it's simply that grief changes over time."

"In my experience," Thomas said quietly, "grief never truly leaves us. But it does become... more manageable. Like a wound that heals but leaves a scar."

There was something in his tone that made Nell look at him more closely.

"You speak from experience."

Thomas didn't look at her. "I lost my entire unit in Spain," he said. "Good men. Better than I deserved to lead."

Nell stepped closer, the snow crunching beneath her boots. "That isn't your fault."

He met her gaze then—unflinching, wounded. "Isn't it?"

This, Nell thought, *is what grief looks like in a man who hasn't let himself weep.*

The stark admission hung between them, and Nell felt her heart clench at the pain beneath his matter-of-fact delivery. So that was the shape of his grief—discipline, silence, control. Not so different from her own, she realized, though manifested differently.

"I'm sorry," she said, inadequate though the words were.

Thomas straightened, shouldering the bundle of evergreen branches with practiced ease. "Thank you. However, my point is that we learn to carry our losses differently over time. They become part of us rather than something that consumes us."

As they made their way back through the snow toward the warmth of the conservatory, Nell found herself seeing Thomas

Greystowe in an entirely new light. The man who had seemed so coldly practical the day before was revealed to have depths of understanding born from his own encounters with loss and responsibility.

As she peeled off her damp gloves, Nell glanced sidelong at the Earl. He'd worked without complaint, offered a steady arm without presumption, and even remembered Isabella's fondness for holly. That last detail struck her unexpectedly—not as a performance, but as the mark of someone who had paid attention, even when no one had expected it of him. It was such a quiet kind of goodness, the kind one rarely noticed until it was gone—or standing beside you with snow in his hair, asking nothing in return.

Perhaps, she thought as they stamped the snow from their boots and stepped back into the conservatory's embrace, being snowbound at Greystowe Hall might not be a hardship after all. Especially when the cold outside made the warmth between them so unmistakable.

CHAPTER 5

Tinsel and Tension

The great hall of Greystowe had been transformed into what could only be described as a battlefield of holiday preparation. Evergreen boughs lay scattered across tables, ribbons in various states of untangling draped over chairs, and an impressive collection of ornaments—some clearly precious family heirlooms, others charmingly handmade—awaited deployment throughout the vast space.

Nell stood in the center of it all, surveying the organized chaos with the eye of a general planning a campaign. She had approached the decoration of the hall with the same thoroughness she brought to any project, but the sheer scale of Greystowe's great room presented challenges she hadn't anticipated at her family's more modest estate.

"I believe we may have been overly ambitious," she admitted to Lady Greystowe, who was seated near the fire with a cup of tea and an expression of serene satisfaction.

"Nonsense, my dear. It simply requires a proper strategy."

Lady Greystowe gestured toward the soaring stone fireplace that dominated one end of the hall. "Start with the mantelpiece as your focal point, then work outward. Thomas should be along shortly to assist with the higher placements."

As if summoned by his aunt's words, Thomas appeared in the doorway, surveying the scene with what Nell was beginning to recognize as his standard assessment expression. Today, however, she thought she detected a hint of amusement beneath his military bearing.

"I see you've mobilized for a full-scale assault on Christmas decoration," he observed, stepping carefully around a particularly elaborate garland that had somehow migrated to the floor.

"Your aunt believes in thoroughness," Nell replied, attempting to untangle a particularly stubborn length of ribbon. "Though I'm beginning to suspect she may have overestimated my organizational capabilities."

"Unlikely." Thomas moved to assist her with the ribbon, his fingers working with surprising dexterity to free the silk from its knots. "From what I observed yesterday, your capabilities are quite impressive when properly applied."

Nell arched a brow. "A rare compliment, my lord."

"Not so rare," he murmured, glancing toward the tall window that overlooked the front drive. "I once spent a week convincing my commanding officer that a half-frozen terrier was a suitable regimental mascot."

"Did he agree?"

"He relented. The dog outranked several lieutenants by the end of the year."

Nell laughed, caught off guard by the warmth in his voice. "I wouldn't have imagined you the sentimental sort."

CHRISTMAS WITH THE EARL

"I'm not," he replied evenly. "But some things deserve loyalty."

The compliment, delivered in his matter-of-fact tone, brought a warm bloom to Nell's cheeks. She found herself studying his hands as he worked—strong, capable hands that bore small scars from his military service but moved with surprising gentleness when handling delicate things.

"There," he said, presenting her with the freed ribbon. "Though I confess I'm not entirely certain what comes next in this particular campaign."

"The mantelpiece," Nell said, grateful to have a concrete task to focus on. "Lady Greystowe suggests we begin there and work outward."

"A sound strategy. Secure your stronghold first, then expand your territory." Thomas gathered an armload of evergreen boughs and moved toward the massive fireplace. "I assume you have a vision for how this should appear when completed?"

Nell followed him, her own arms full of holly and ivy. "Something elegant but welcoming. Not too formal, but befitting the grandeur of the space." She paused, considering. "Isabella always said Christmas decorations should make a room feel like home, regardless of how grand it might be."

Thomas had climbed onto a chair to reach the higher portions of the mantelpiece, but he paused at her words. "She had a gift for making places feel welcoming. Even during the brief time I knew her, that was evident."

Nell smiled faintly. "Yes, she was everyone's bright star."

Thomas glanced at her, something unreadable flickering across his face. "Some stars burn too brightly to last."

She froze. Was that meant as sympathy or judgment? The

thought unsettled her more than she cared to admit. She bent over a bundle of ivy, grateful for the distraction.

"Did you visit often when she was alive?" Nell asked, surprising herself with her boldness.

"Only once, I'm ashamed to say," Thomas replied, arranging branches along the stone shelf with a note of regret. "Military duties kept me away more than I'd have liked. I missed a great deal of family happiness during those years."

Thomas's voice carried a note of regret as he arranged branches along the stone shelf. "Military duties kept me away more than I would have liked. I rather suspect I missed a great deal of family happiness during those years."

Something in his tone made Nell look up at him more closely. There was a wistfulness in his expression that she hadn't seen before, a suggestion that his absence from Greystowe Hall had been as much a loss as a duty.

"Well, you're here now," she said gently. "That must count for something."

Thomas glanced down at her, and for a moment, their eyes met and held. There was something unguarded in his expression, a vulnerability that made her breath catch slightly.

"Yes," he said quietly. "I suppose it does."

The moment stretched between them, filled with an awareness that had nothing to do with Christmas decorations and everything to do with the slow shift in understanding that had been building since their expedition into the snow.

"If you two are quite finished having a moment," Lady Greystowe's voice cut through their reverie with obvious amusement, "I believe the ivy requires attention before it wilts entirely."

Nell felt heat flood her cheeks as she turned back to her work, but not before she caught sight of Thomas's slightly reddened ears as he resumed his own task with perhaps more vigor than necessary.

"Of course," Nell managed, focusing intently on the arrangement of ivy leaves as though it were the most crucial task in the world. "The ivy. Absolutely."

For the next hour, they worked in companionable efficiency, with Thomas handling the higher placements while Nell managed the more detailed arrangements at eye level. Lady Greystowe provided commentary and suggestions from her chair by the fire, occasionally rising to inspect their progress with the air of a benevolent commanding officer.

The work itself proved surprisingly enjoyable. Thomas's systematic approach complemented Nell's artistic instincts, and they developed an easy rhythm of communication—a gesture here, a brief consultation there, an occasional shared smile when a particularly stubborn branch finally cooperated.

"The garland along the staircase will require both of you," Lady Greystowe announced when they had finished with the mantelpiece. "The banister is too long for one person to manage alone, and the draping must be even if it's to look proper."

Nell eyed the sweeping staircase that curved gracefully to the upper floors. The banister was indeed impressive—polished oak that gleamed in the firelight—but the prospect of decorating its entire length seemed daunting.

"We'll need to coordinate our efforts," Thomas said, following her gaze. "You take one end, I'll take the other, and we'll work toward the middle."

"That sounds reasonable," Nell agreed, though she was already anticipating the logistical challenges. "Though we'll need to maintain consistent spacing, or the effect will be uneven."

"Naturally." Thomas gathered up the longest of their prepared garlands, testing its weight and flexibility. "Military operations have taught me the importance of precise coordination."

"This is hardly a military operation," Nell pointed out with amusement.

"You'd be surprised how many principles apply," Thomas replied with what she was almost certain was a hint of a smile. "Preparation, coordination, and adaptability when circumstances change unexpectedly."

"And what happens when circumstances change unexpectedly in Christmas decorating?"

"Improvisation," Thomas said promptly. "And occasionally, strategic retreat."

Despite herself, Nell laughed. "I shall keep that in mind should we encounter any decorative emergencies."

They positioned themselves at opposite ends of the banister and began the careful process of draping the garland. It required constant communication—"A bit higher on your end," "Can you give me more length here?" "How does the spacing look from your angle?"—and more coordination than Nell had anticipated.

The real challenge came when they reached the curve in the staircase where the banister swept in an elegant arc. Suddenly, they found themselves working in much closer proximity, having to pass the garland back and forth while navigating around each other in the confined space.

"If you could just..." Thomas began, reaching around her to adjust the draping.

"I think it needs to..." Nell started at the same moment, turning directly into his path.

They collided gently, Thomas's steadying hands catching her waist while hers instinctively came up to rest against his chest. For a moment, they stood frozen in an inadvertent embrace, the forgotten garland draped around them both like some sort of Christmas conspiracy.

Nell found herself looking up into Thomas's gray eyes, noting the way they seemed darker in the shadows of the staircase, the way his breath created small puffs of warmth in the cooler air near the windows. She was acutely aware of the solid strength of his chest beneath her palms, the way his hands remained steady at her waist as though he were reluctant to let her go.

"I..." she began, though she had no idea what she intended to say.

"Yes," Thomas replied, as though she had asked a question rather than stammered an incomplete thought.

His voice was quiet, but there was something in it—something unspoken and tentative—that made her wonder what exactly he had answered.

The sound of slow, deliberate applause from the direction of the fireplace broke the spell. They sprang apart as though the garland had caught fire, both turning to see Lady Greystowe watching them with an expression of poorly concealed delight.

"Beautifully executed," she said with perfect composure. "Though I believe the garland may require some adjustment after that... collaboration."

Nell felt as though her face might actually combust from embarrassment. She bent quickly to retrieve the scattered greenery, grateful for the excuse to avoid looking at either Thomas or his aunt.

"Quite right," Thomas said, his voice carefully neutral—though Nell caught that faint catch, that near-mistake he didn't quite cover. "We should... that is, the garland..."

Lady Greystowe, ever the master of timing, chose that moment to speak. "Indeed. Though I daresay, if your collaboration becomes any more... spirited, we may need to hang mistletoe after all."

The word 'mistletoe' seemed to hang in the air with as much significance as the plant itself might have done. Nell risked a glance at Thomas and found him looking directly at her with an expression she couldn't quite interpret—part amusement, part something else entirely.

"I believe," Thomas said carefully, "that we should focus on completing our current decorations before considering additional... botanical elements."

"Of course," Lady Greystowe replied, but her smile suggested she found the entire situation thoroughly satisfactory. "Though I do think we've made excellent progress for one morning. Perhaps we might continue after luncheon?"

As they gathered their materials and prepared to retire to the dining room, Nell found herself stealing glances at Thomas. The easy camaraderie of their morning's work had shifted into something more complex, more charged with possibilities she wasn't entirely sure she was ready to examine.

But as they walked toward the dining room, Thomas fell into step beside her, and when their shoulders brushed briefly in the doorway, neither of them moved away.

Perhaps, Nell thought, some possibilities were worth exploring after all.

CHAPTER 6

A Walk in the Snow

T he storm that had raged through the night finally
exhausted itself sometime before dawn, leaving behind
a world transformed. When Nell woke to brilliant
sunlight streaming through the frost-etched windows of the Blue
Room, she could hardly believe the sight that greeted her.

The sky had cleared to a crystalline blue that seemed almost
impossibly vivid against the pristine white landscape. Every surface
sparkled with fresh snow that caught the morning light like scattered diamonds. The oppressive weight of the previous day's bliz-
zard had lifted, replaced by a crisp clarity that made the air itself
seem to shimmer with possibility.

She dressed quickly in her warmest wool gown—a deep forest
green that Isabella had always said brought out the color of her
eyes—and made her way downstairs to find the household already
stirring with the energy that comes after surviving nature's fury.

Mrs. Hartwell greeted her in the breakfast room with the satisfied air of a general whose defenses had held against siege. "Good morning, my lady. Cook's managed a proper hot breakfast despite yesterday's excitement, and his lordship's already been out assessing the damage to the grounds."

"Damage?" Nell asked with concern, accepting the steaming cup of chocolate the housekeeper offered.

"Oh, nothing serious, my lady. A few branches down from the weight of the snow, and one of the garden gates will need mending where the wind caught it. But the house stood firm, as she always has." Mrs. Hartwell's pride in Greystowe Hall was evident in every word. "His lordship seems quite impressed with how well the estate weathered the storm."

Nell found herself unexpectedly pleased by this news. She had seen the way Thomas looked at the property with his assessor's eye, calculating costs and liabilities rather than appreciating its enduring strength. Perhaps witnessing the Hall's resilience in the face of Yorkshire's worst would help him see it as his aunt did— not as a burden, but as a legacy worth preserving.

She was contemplating this possibility over her breakfast when Lady Greystowe appeared, already dressed for the day and wearing an expression of barely contained excitement.

"My dear Eleanor, what a glorious morning! I do believe the worst of the weather has passed, and Thomas has confirmed that the immediate grounds are quite safe for walking." Lady Greystowe settled herself with her tea, but her energy was clearly focused on something beyond mere meteorological observations. "I thought perhaps you might enjoy exploring the winter gardens properly, now that we can venture out without fear of being swept away by the wind."

"That sounds delightful," Nell replied, though she couldn't

shake the feeling that Lady Greystowe's suggestion came with ulterior motives. "Though I confess I'm not certain I have appropriate footwear for such deep snow."

"Oh, that's easily remedied. Isabella kept several pairs of winter boots, and you're much the same size. I'm sure we can find something suitable." Lady Greystowe's smile held that familiar glint of mischief. "And of course, Thomas has offered to serve as guide and protection against any treacherous patches. So thoughtful of him, don't you think?"

Before Nell could formulate a response to this transparent bit of matchmaking, the man in question appeared in the doorway, stamping snow from his boots and bringing with him the crisp scent of winter air. Wind had disheveled his hair; the cold left color high on his cheeks, and there was an energy about him that she hadn't seen before, as though the storm's passage had swept away some invisible weight he'd been carrying.

"Good morning," he said, his gaze moving directly to Nell with a warmth that made her pulse quicken. "I trust you slept well despite the wind? The house can be rather dramatic in such weather."

"Very well, thank you," Nell managed, trying not to notice how the morning light caught the gray of his eyes, making them seem almost silver. "Mrs. Hartwell tells me you've been surveying the estate. No serious damage, I hope?"

"Nothing that cannot be easily repaired," Thomas replied, moving to warm his hands by the fire. "The old oak near the east garden lost a large branch, but it was diseased and needed to come down anyway. If anything, the storm did us a favor by removing it safely."

There was something different in his tone when he spoke of

the estate's welfare—a proprietary concern that suggested he was beginning to think of Greystowe Hall as more than just property to be assessed and potentially disposed of.

"Aunt Margaret mentioned you might be interested in seeing the winter gardens," he continued, his attention returning to Nell. "The snow has created some rather spectacular effects, if you don't mind the cold."

"I would love to see them," Nell said, surprised by how readily the words came. The prospect of walking through the winter landscape with Thomas as her guide held an appeal that had nothing to do with botanical interest and everything to do with the way he was looking at her. He looked as though her company would be a pleasure rather than an obligation.

"Splendid," Lady Greystowe declared before Nell could second-guess her enthusiasm. "I shall have Isabella's boots brought down, and you can wrap up warmly. The fresh air will do you both good after being confined indoors."

Half an hour later, Nell found herself bundled in a wool cloak with Isabella's boots, which did indeed fit perfectly, laced snugly around her ankles. Thomas waited by the conservatory door, similarly attired for winter weather, though his military bearing made even the most practical clothing seem somehow elegant.

"Ready for your expedition?" he asked, offering his arm with a formality that was belied by the anticipation in his expression.

"Ready," Nell confirmed, accepting his escort and trying to ignore the way her pulse jumped at the contact.

They stepped out into the transformed world, and Nell's breath caught at the beauty that surrounded them. The formal gardens had become something from a fairy tale, with every hedge and pathway transformed by the snow into graceful curves and mysterious shadows. The bare branches of the trees created intricate lacework against the blue sky, and the fountain at the center of the rose garden had become a sculpture of ice and snow that seemed to capture movement in crystalline stillness.

"It's magnificent," she breathed, unconsciously tightening her grip on Thomas's arm as she tried to take in every detail.

"Isabella always said winter was when Greystowe showed its true character," Thomas replied, his voice carrying a warmth that spoke of genuine affection for the memory. "She claimed the snow revealed the garden's bones, the underlying structure that made it beautiful in every season."

They walked slowly along what Nell gradually realized must be the main garden path, though it was invisible beneath the pristine snow. Thomas guided her with sure steps, his knowledge of the grounds evident in the way he anticipated hidden obstacles and chose the safest route.

"You know the estate well," Nell observed, impressed by his confidence in the terrain.

"I spent summers here as a boy," Thomas replied, pausing to help her navigate around a snow-covered bench. "Before my father decided I needed the discipline of military school. I used to know every path, every hiding place, every tree suitable for climbing." His voice carried a note of nostalgia that softened his usual crisp delivery. "It's been interesting to discover how much I still remember."

They had reached the rose garden, where the careful geometry of the beds was outlined in snow and the arbor entrance stood draped in icicles like nature's own crystal chandelier. Isabella had once written of this very spot in winter, describing how the arbor looked like a palace gate carved from ice. Seeing it now, Nell understood her sister's enchantment—and felt a bittersweet pang that was somehow more healing than painful.

Thomas paused, his gaze moving across the winter landscape with an expression that mingled memory and something that might have been longing.

"Do you ever regret choosing the military?" Nell asked softly, struck by the wistfulness in his expression.

Thomas was quiet for a long moment, his breath creating small clouds in the crisp air as he considered her question. "I thought it was what I wanted," he said finally. "Order, purpose, a clear chain of command. No messy emotions or complicated family obligations." He glanced at her, and she saw something vulnerable in his eyes. "I told myself that sentiment was a luxury I couldn't afford."

"And now?"

"Now I find myself questioning whether I was running toward something or away from it." Thomas's confession came quietly, as though the words surprised him as much as they did her.

They continued walking, following what must have been the path toward the wilderness gardens. Here, the landscape became less formal, more natural, with stands of evergreens that had caught the snow in their branches like nature's own Christmas decorations. The silence between them was comfortable, filled with the soft crunch of their footsteps and the occasional whisper of wind through the snow-laden boughs.

When they reached a slight rise that offered a view back toward the house, Thomas stopped, and Nell found herself looking at Greystowe Hall as though seeing it for the first time. From this vantage point, the ancient stone walls seemed to glow in the morning sunlight, and smoke rising from the chimneys spoke of warmth and life within. It looked like a place where people belonged, where families had found happiness for generations.

"I used to come here when I needed to think," Thomas said, following her gaze. "There's something about seeing the house from this distance that puts things in perspective."

"What sort of things?" Nell asked, though she thought she might already understand. There was something about the view that made the estate seem less like property and more like home.

"Whether duty and practicality are always the same thing," Thomas replied. "Whether preserving something beautiful is worth the cost, even when the numbers don't quite add up."

Nell turned to study his profile, noting the way his expression had softened as he looked at his inherited home. "And what conclusion have you reached?"

"That perhaps I've been asking the wrong questions," Thomas said, his voice carrying a note of revelation. "I've been calculating whether I can afford to keep Greystowe Hall. I should have been asking whether I can afford to lose it."

Nell turned to him. "You said there's a deadline."

He gave a short nod. "If I do not take formal possession—by way of proving occupancy and solvency—before Twelfth Night, some of the peripheral lands may be sold to satisfy the clause in the entail. The Hall itself would remain, for now. But stripped of its farming income, it would become a liability. A hollow shell."

She was quiet for a moment. "Then this place depends on your decision."

"As do others. Tenants, staff, my aunt... all waiting to see whether I choose to keep a legacy I never asked for."

The admission hung between them, and Nell felt her heart clench at the pain beneath his practical words. "Perhaps," Nell said, "it's not about what you asked for, but what you might deserve."

Here was a man who had trained himself to value duty over desire, responsibility over sentiment, and yet the sight of his family's home in its winter beauty was threatening to undo all those careful defenses.

"It would be a tremendous loss," she said gently. "Not just for your family, but for everyone who has found happiness here." The words 'including me' hovered on her lips, but she caught herself, startled by how readily the thought had formed.

Thomas turned to look at her then, and there was something in his expression that made her breath catch. "I'm beginning to understand that," he said quietly. "Though I confess I'm not entirely sure what to do with the understanding."

Nell hesitated, her gloved hands clasped in front of her.

"You said something once," she murmured, not quite meeting his gaze. "About stars burning too brightly."

Thomas tilted his head. "Did I?"

"Yes. When we were decorating. I thought you meant—" she paused, her voice tight. "That I was only ever going to be a poor imitation of Isabella."

The wind stirred a drift behind them, but neither moved.

"No," he said quietly, but with the clarity of someone who meant to be understood. "I meant she never saw the edge of things coming. You do. You guard yourself. That's not weakness, Eleanor. It's the reason you're still standing."

Nell exhaled, something between a sigh and a release. The ache she hadn't named loosened its grip.

They stood there in the crisp morning air, two people who had found themselves in circumstances neither had expected, looking at a house that somehow represented possibilities neither had dared to consider. The snow sparkled around them like scattered stars, and the silence stretched with the weight of things unspoken.

It was Thomas who finally broke the spell, though his voice was gentler than usual. "We should head back. I'm certain your hands are beginning to turn blue, and Aunt Margaret will never forgive me if I allow you to take a chill."

Nell looked down at her gloved hands, surprised to realize she had indeed grown quite cold without noticing. But as Thomas offered his arm again, she was acutely aware that the warmth spreading through her had nothing to do with the prospect of returning to the house's heated rooms.

As they retraced their steps through the snow, walking closer together now against the cold, Nell found herself stealing glances at Thomas. The rigid military bearing she had first encountered was still there, but softened somehow by their morning's expedition. He moved through his family's grounds with a growing sense of belonging that seemed to surprise him as much as it pleased her.

When they paused at a particularly icy patch where the path curved around a fountain, Thomas tightened his grip on her arm, his other hand coming up to steady her waist as she navigated the treacherous footing. For a moment, they were very close, close enough that she could see the individual snowflakes caught in his dark hair, close enough to notice the way his breathing had quickened despite the leisurely pace of their walk.

"Careful," he murmured, but his hands remained at her waist even after she had found her footing, as though he were reluctant to let her go.

Nell found herself looking up into his gray eyes, noting the way they seemed to reflect the winter light, the way his gaze seemed to linger on her face as though memorizing every detail. There was something in the air between them—awareness, possibility, the faint tremor of connection that neither was quite ready to acknowledge aloud.

"Thank you," she managed, though the words came out breathier than she intended.

"My pleasure," Thomas replied, and there was something in his tone that suggested he meant far more than simple politeness.

They remained frozen for a heartbeat longer, hands connected, breath mingling in the cold air, the silence between them heavy with possibility, before Thomas seemed to catch himself and stepped back with careful deliberation.

"The house," he said, his voice slightly rougher than usual. "We should... that is, the warmth..."

"Yes," Nell agreed quickly, though she felt oddly bereft when his hands dropped away. "Lady Greystowe will be wondering what's become of us."

As they completed their walk back to the conservatory, both carefully maintaining proper distance now, Nell couldn't shake the feeling that something significant had shifted between them. The barriers Thomas had maintained so carefully were showing cracks, and the glimpses of the man beneath his defenses were proving dangerously appealing.

When they finally stepped back into the conservatory's welcome warmth, Thomas helped her remove her cloak with the same careful attention he might have given a precious artifact. Their fingers brushed as he lifted the heavy wool from her shoulders, and Nell felt that same jolt of awareness that had marked their moment by the fountain.

"Eleanor, Thomas, there you are!" Lady Greystowe's voice carried from the doorway, though Nell thought she detected a note of satisfaction beneath the maternal concern. "You both look wonderfully refreshed. I trust the gardens were worth the expedition?"

"Very much so," Nell replied, working to keep her voice steady as she avoided Thomas's gaze. "The winter beauty is really quite extraordinary."

"Indeed," Thomas agreed, his tone carefully neutral, though Nell noticed he was having similar difficulty with normal conversation. "Most... illuminating."

Lady Greystowe's smile suggested she had heard far more in their responses than either had intended to reveal. "Splendid. Well then, perhaps you'd both like some hot chocolate by the fire? Cook has prepared a lovely luncheon, and I thought we might continue our discussion about tomorrow's Christmas Eve preparations."

As they made their way toward the house proper, Nell found herself acutely aware of Thomas walking beside her. The morning's expedition had revealed layers to his character she hadn't suspected, and the growing warmth in his manner toward both her and Greystowe Hall suggested possibilities she wasn't entirely sure she was prepared to examine.

But as they settled by the drawing room fire with steaming cups of chocolate, and Lady Greystowe began outlining her plans for Christmas Eve dinner, Nell caught Thomas watching her with an expression of quiet thoughtfulness that made her pulse quicken with anticipation for whatever revelations the day might yet bring.

Outside, fresh snow had begun to fall again, but gently this time—not the fierce storm of confinement, but the soft blessing of a world being made new.

CHAPTER 7
Christmas Eve Supper

The drawing room at Greystowe Hall had been transformed for Christmas Eve. Candles flickered from every available surface—tall tapers in silver holders, squat pillars nestled among evergreen boughs, and delicate votives that cast dancing shadows across the ancient stone walls. The scent of pine and holly mingled with the warmth of applewood burning in the great hearth, creating an atmosphere that seemed to wrap around the small gathering like an embrace.

Nell stood before the looking glass in the Blue Room, adjusting the simple strand of pearls at her throat with hands that trembled slightly. She had chosen her finest black silk—appropriate for her mourning, yet elegant enough for Lady Greystowe's carefully planned evening. The gown's cut was becoming without being ostentatious, and she had allowed her maid to arrange her dark hair in a softer style than usual, with gentle curls framing her face.

It was only the three of them for dinner, yet Nell felt an anticipation that had nothing to do with the meal and everything to do with the way Thomas had looked at her during their morning walk. Something had shifted between them in the snow-covered gardens, some barrier had begun to crack, and she found herself both yearning for and terrified of what the evening might reveal.

A soft knock interrupted her nervous preparations. "Come in," she called.

Lady Greystowe entered, resplendent in deep burgundy silk with her late husband's garnets at her throat and ears. In her hands, she carried a small velvet box that seemed to glow in the candlelight.

"My dear," Lady Greystowe said, her voice carrying an unusual note of emotion, "you look absolutely lovely."

"Thank you," Nell replied, though her attention was drawn to the box in the older woman's hands. "Is that...?"

"Something I hoped you might wear tonight." Lady Greystowe moved closer, opening the box to reveal a pendant that made Nell's breath catch in her throat. It was a delicate thing—a small oval of amber set in gold filigree, suspended from a fine chain that caught the light like captured sunbeams.

"It's exquisite," Nell breathed, but something in Lady Greystowe's expression suggested this was more than mere jewelry.

"It belonged to Isabella," Lady Greystowe said gently. "She wore it on her wedding day, and often during the happiest moments of her time here. When she..." The older woman's voice caught slightly. "Before she died, she asked me to give it to someone who would bring joy back to Greystowe Hall."

Nell felt tears prick her eyes as she looked at the pendant. To wear something of Isabella's felt both like an honor and a responsibility she wasn't certain she could bear.

"I couldn't possibly—" she began, but Lady Greystowe stepped forward with the determined air of someone who would not be refused.

"She specifically mentioned you, my dear. Said that if anything happened to her, I should remember that you had the gift of bringing light to dark places." Lady Greystowe's hands were gentle but firm as she lifted the chain. "May I?"

Nell nodded, too moved to speak, and bowed her head to allow Lady Greystowe to fasten the pendant around her neck. The amber felt warm against her skin, as though it carried some echo of her sister's spirit.

"There," Lady Greystowe said with satisfaction, stepping back to admire the effect. "Perfect. Isabella would be so pleased to see you wearing it."

Before Nell could respond, they were interrupted by the sound of masculine footsteps in the corridor. Thomas's voice carried clearly as he spoke to his valet about some detail of his evening attire.

"He's been rather particular about his appearance tonight," Lady Greystowe observed with obvious amusement. "I believe he's changed his cravat three times. Most unusual for a man who typically approaches dress with military efficiency."

The implications of this information sent a flutter of anticipation through Nell's stomach. If Thomas was taking special care with his appearance, it suggested the evening held significance for him as well.

When they made their way downstairs, they found the dining room had been prepared with equal attention to beauty and intimacy. The long table had been abandoned in favor of a smaller round table positioned near the fireplace, set for three with the finest china and crystal. More candles provided the only illumination, creating pools of golden light that made the room feel like a jewel box.

Thomas stood near the fireplace, and Nell's breath caught at the sight of him. He wore evening dress with the same precision he brought to everything else, but there was something different about his bearing tonight. The rigid military posture had softened slightly, and when he turned to greet them, his smile held a warmth that reached his eyes.

"Ladies," he said, offering formal bows that somehow managed to convey both respect and affection. "You both look radiant this evening."

His gaze lingered on Nell, and she saw the exact moment when he noticed the pendant. Something flickered across his expression—recognition, perhaps, or surprise—before his features settled into something that might have been gratitude.

"Aunt Margaret," he said quietly, "that's Isabella's pendant."

"Indeed, it is," Lady Greystowe replied with perfect composure. "I thought it belonged with someone who would honor its history while creating new memories."

The look that passed between Thomas and his aunt spoke of understanding that went beyond words. Then his attention returned to Nell, and there was something in his expression that made her pulse quicken.

"It suits you," he said simply, but there was a depth to his voice that suggested layers of meaning beneath the polite observation.

The meal that followed was unlike any Nell had experienced since Isabella's death. Cook had outdone himself despite the reduced household—delicate soup flavored with herbs from the estate's gardens, perfectly roasted fowl with winter vegetables, and a delicate syllabub that tasted of Christmas itself. But more than the food, it was the atmosphere that enchanted her.

Lady Greystowe proved herself a masterful hostess, guiding conversation through topics that allowed all three to contribute while never letting the mood grow heavy or awkward. She drew out stories of Thomas's boyhood summers at Greystowe, encouraged Nell to share memories of Christmas traditions at her family's estate, and somehow managed to weave their separate histories into something that felt like the beginning of a shared narrative.

"I remember one Christmas when Thomas was perhaps ten," Lady Greystowe said as they lingered over their wine, "he decided the estate needed a proper Yule log and dragged in something that was practically a small tree. It took four footmen to get it into the fireplace, and it burned for nearly a week."

"I was very thorough in my approach to Christmas traditions," Thomas replied with what Nell was almost certain was embarrassment. "I had read that the Yule log should burn continuously until Twelfth Night."

"And did it?" Nell asked, delighted by this glimpse of Thomas as an earnest boy taking his holiday responsibilities seriously.

"Nearly. Though I believe Cook threatened to quit when the smoke made the entire house smell like a forest fire for days." Thomas's smile held genuine fondness for the memory. "I was devastated when they finally had to remove what remained. I was certain I had failed in my duty to ensure proper Christmas luck for the household."

"Such a serious child," Lady Greystowe said with affection. "Always so concerned with doing everything correctly, with living up to expectations."

"Some things never change," Thomas observed wryly, but

there was something in his tone that suggested he was beginning to question whether living up to expectations was always the highest virtue.

As the evening progressed, Nell found herself watching Thomas with growing fascination. Away from the formality of day clothes and surrounded by candlelight and family affection, he seemed younger, more relaxed. His laugh came more easily, his smiles were less guarded, and there were moments when she glimpsed the boy who had worried about Yule logs and Christmas luck.

When they moved to the drawing room for coffee and the small gifts Lady Greystowe had prepared, the intimate atmosphere only deepened. She had clearly planned this evening with care— small presents that spoke of thoughtfulness rather than expense, carefully chosen to honor their individual tastes while binding them together as a temporary family.

For Thomas, she had found a leather-bound volume of poetry that had belonged to his father. For Nell, a delicate set of water-colors that she claimed had been gathering dust in the estate's art supplies, but were clearly of excellent quality. And for herself, she accepted a beautifully bound journal that Thomas had somehow procured despite their confinement—a testament to his resource-fulness and growing affection for his aunt.

"I thought you might enjoy recording your observations about estate management," Thomas said as Lady Greystowe examined the journal with obvious pleasure. "Your insights have been... illu-minating during my assessment."

It was a diplomatic way of saying that his aunt's perspective had changed his understanding of Greystowe Hall, and Nell saw Lady Greystowe's satisfied smile at the admission.

"Now then," Lady Greystowe said, settling herself more comfortably in her chair, "I believe Christmas Eve calls for a reading. Eleanor, my dear, would you honor us with something from that poetry collection Isabella loved so much?"

Nell felt the familiar tightness in her chest at the mention of her sister, but it was gentler now, less sharp than it had been. She retrieved the small volume she had been carrying with her since arriving at Greystowe—Isabella's own copy of Christmas poems, its pages soft with handling and marked with her sister's careful annotations.

"She particularly loved this one," Nell said, finding the familiar page. The poem was one of gentle celebration, speaking of winter's beauty and the warmth found in gathering with those we love. As she read, her voice growing stronger with each verse, she became aware of the perfect stillness in the room. Even the fire seemed to burn more quietly, as though nature itself wished to listen.

When she finished, the silence that followed was not empty but full, pregnant with shared emotion and the sense of Isabella's presence blessing their small celebration.

"Beautiful," Thomas said quietly, and when Nell looked up, she found his gaze fixed on her with an intensity that made her heart skip. "She chose well."

"In all things," Lady Greystowe added softly, and Nell had the distinct impression that she was speaking of more than literary taste.

As the evening drew toward its close, Lady Greystowe rose with the grace of someone making a carefully planned exit. "I believe I shall retire now and leave you young people to enjoy the fire. Thomas, perhaps you would see that Eleanor has everything she needs for her comfort?"

The suggestion was delivered with such perfect innocence that it took a moment for its implications to register. They were being deliberately left alone, and from the satisfied glint in Lady Greystowe's eyes, this had been her intention all along.

"Certainly," Thomas replied, though Nell noticed a slight tension in his voice that suggested he, too, had grasped his aunt's purpose.

After Lady Greystowe departed with wishes for sweet dreams and Christmas blessings, Nell found herself alone with Thomas in the candlelit drawing room. The fire had burned down to glowing embers, and the only sounds were the soft tick of the mantle clock and the gentle whisper of snow against the windows.

"More coffee?" Thomas asked, his voice carrying a formality that seemed at odds with the intimate atmosphere Lady Greystowe had so carefully created.

"Thank you," Nell replied, though she made no move to drink from the cup he handed her. Instead, she found herself studying his profile as he resumed his seat, noting the way the firelight played across his features and softened the hard lines that military life had carved there.

"It's been a lovely evening," she said finally, when the silence threatened to become awkward.

"Yes," Thomas agreed, but his tone was distracted, as though his thoughts were elsewhere. He was looking at the pendant at her throat, she realized, his expression unreadable in the dim light.

"She would have liked seeing you wear that," he said suddenly, his voice soft but clear. "Isabella, I mean. She had very definite opinions about people, about who belonged where and with whom."

There was something in his tone that made Nell set down her coffee cup and give him her full attention. "What sort of opinions?"

Thomas was quiet for a long moment, seeming to gather his thoughts with the same systematic approach he brought to military planning. When he finally spoke, his words came slowly, as though he were testing each one before giving it voice.

"She wrote to me, you know. During the last months, when she was... when she knew the birth would be difficult." His voice caught slightly, but he continued. "She spoke of you often. Said you had a gift for bringing comfort to dark places, for making people feel less alone in their sorrows."

Nell felt tears prick her eyes at this unexpected revelation. "She never told me she was corresponding with you."

"I think she was trying to prepare me," Thomas said quietly. "For the possibility that things might not end well. She wanted to be sure that those she loved would not be left entirely alone with their grief."

The admission hung between them, heavy with implication. Here was Thomas acknowledging not just his cousin's death, but his own loss—and perhaps, Nell dared to hope, suggesting that she had somehow helped heal that wound.

"She also said," Thomas continued, his voice growing even quieter, "that when I finally returned to Greystowe, I should pay attention to who made the house feel like home again."

Nell's breath caught at the words, at their possible meaning. The pendant at her throat seemed to grow warmer, as though

Isabella's spirit was somehow present in the room, blessing what-ever understanding was growing between them.

"Thomas," she began, but he held up a hand, his expression serious.

"I came here to assess whether Greystowe Hall was worth preserving," he said, his gray eyes meeting hers directly. "I thought it was a question of finances, of practical considerations versus sentimental attachment."

"And now?" Nell asked, though her heart was beating so loudly she was amazed he couldn't hear it.

"Now I understand that the real question was never about the house at all," Thomas replied. "It was about whether I was brave enough to stop running from the possibility of belonging some-where. Of belonging to someone."

The words hung in the candlelit air between them, heavy with meaning and possibility. Nell felt as though she stood at the edge of a precipice—one step forward would change everything, but she wasn't certain she had the courage to take it.

"The house feels different when you're here," Thomas contin-ued, his voice barely above a whisper. "Warmer. More alive. More like the home I remember from childhood rather than the burden I inherited."

"Thomas," Nell said again, and this time her voice carried a note of warning. "You must be careful what you say. I am still in mourning, still finding my way through grief. I cannot—"

"I'm not asking you to do anything but listen," Thomas inter-rupted gently. "I know this is neither the time nor the place for... for what I might wish to say under different circumstances. But I needed you to know that your presence here has meant more than comfort. It has meant hope."

The fire crackled softly in the silence that followed, and Nell found herself studying Thomas's face in the golden light. There was vulnerability there, carefully controlled but unmistakable. Here was a man who had spent years building walls around his heart, and those walls were crumbling in the face of possibilities he had never allowed himself to consider.

"When your mourning period ends," Thomas said finally, "when you are ready to consider your future... I hope you might remember this evening. Remember that there is a place here for you, should you choose to claim it."

It was not quite a proposal, not quite a declaration, but something more tentative and infinitely more precious—an offer of possibility, a promise of patience, a recognition that some things were worth waiting for.

"I will remember," Nell whispered, her hand moving instinctively to the pendant at her throat. "All of it."

They sat in comfortable silence then, watching the fire burn down to embers while snow continued to fall outside the windows. Neither spoke of love directly, but it was there in the room with them—gentle, patient, and full of promise for whatever the future might bring.

When Thomas finally escorted her to the foot of the stairs, his hand lingered on hers for just a moment longer than propriety demanded.

"Merry Christmas, Eleanor," he said softly.

"Merry Christmas, Thomas," she replied, and then, with a courage that surprised them both, she rose on her toes and pressed a gentle kiss to his cheek before disappearing up the stairs.

Thomas stood in the darkened hall long after her footsteps

had faded, one hand touching the spot where her lips had briefly warmed his skin, and smiled into the darkness.

Outside, the snow continued to fall—not the fierce storm of confinement, but the gentle blessing of a world being made new.

CHAPTER 8

The Earl's Offer

N ell woke on Christmas morning to the sound of church bells carried on the crisp winter air. For a moment, she lay still in the warmth of her bed, savoring the memory of the previous evening—Thomas's careful words, the weight of Isabella's pendant against her throat, and the tender kiss she had dared to press to his cheek before fleeing to the safety of her chambers.

Had she been too bold? The question had tormented her through the long hours of the night, alternating with moments of breathless wonder at the possibility that Thomas might truly care for her as more than just a welcome guest or a reminder of his beloved cousin.

The pendant lay on her nightstand where she had carefully placed it before retiring, its amber surface catching the morning light that streamed through her windows. Isabella's gift, for surely it had been Isabella's intention all along, was conveyed through Lady Greystowe's loving hands. The thought offered comfort, tempered, however, by an unspoken weight of duty. If her sister had somehow orchestrated this connection from beyond the grave, what obligations did that create?

A soft knock interrupted her contemplation. "Come in," she called, expecting her breakfast tray.

Instead, a young maid she didn't recognize entered with obvious excitement barely contained beneath proper deference. "Begging your pardon, my lady, but there's been a delivery from the village. A basket, my lady, and Mrs. Hartwell says it's most unusual for Christmas morning."

"A delivery?" Nell sat up, curious despite her preoccupation with weightier matters. "Who would be abroad in such weather on Christmas Day?"

"Young Tom from the Widow Hartley's cottage, my lady. Says his grandmother sent him especially, snow or no snow, with grateful regards to his lordship." The maid's eyes sparkled with the pleasure of being part of something significant. "Mrs. Hartwell says the whole village is talking about how the new Earl has come home at last."

The words sent a warm flutter through Nell's chest. Thomas was no longer being viewed as a distant heir assessing his inheritance, but as the rightful lord of the manor returning to take his place among his people. The transformation spoke to something fundamental shifting in how he was perceived—and perhaps in how he perceived himself.

After the maid departed, Nell dressed with particular care in her finest day dress—still black for mourning, but made of silk that caught the light beautifully, with jet buttons that gleamed like dark stars. She arranged her hair in the softer style she had adopted since arriving at Greystowe, and after a moment's hesitation, fastened Isabella's pendant around her neck. Whatever the day might bring, she would face it carrying her sister's blessing.

She found Thomas and Lady Greystowe in the breakfast room, both looking remarkably pleased with themselves despite the early hour. A large wicker basket sat on the sideboard, overflowing with what appeared to be humble but heartfelt offerings —preserves in mismatched jars, knitted items that spoke of careful handiwork, and several small items wrapped in brown paper.

"Good morning, my dear," Lady Greystowe said with a brightness that suggested she had slept better than Nell had managed. "I trust you rested well?"

"Very well, thank you," Nell replied, hoping her voice didn't betray the sleepless hours she had spent reliving every moment of their evening together. "I understand there's been some excitement this morning?"

"Word has spread through the village that Thomas is in residence," Lady Greystowe explained, gesturing toward the basket with obvious pleasure. "The Widow Hartley sent her grandson through the snow with tokens of gratitude from several families. It seems your reputation has preceded you, Thomas."

Thomas looked distinctly uncomfortable with the attention, though Nell noticed he was examining the contents of the basket with genuine interest rather than the dismissive assessment she might have expected from their first meeting.

"I've done nothing to merit such generosity," he said, lifting what appeared to be a hand-knit muffler from the collection. "They don't even know me."

"They know you're family," Lady Greystowe corrected gently. "They know you've come home for Christmas, and they remember your father and grandfather with affection. Sometimes that's enough to begin with."

Nell watched Thomas process this information, noting the way his expression softened as he handled each humble gift. These were offerings from people who had little to spare, yet had chosen to share what they had with a lord they hoped might prove worthy of their loyalty.

"Perhaps," Thomas said slowly, "we might return the gesture. Is it not traditional for the estate to provide Christmas gifts to the tenants?"

"Very traditional," Lady Greystowe agreed, though her tone carried a note of surprise at his interest. "Though we've had to reduce the scope in recent years, with the uncertainty about the estate's future."

"What would be appropriate?" Thomas asked, and Nell felt her heart warm at the genuine concern in his voice. "I'm afraid my military experience didn't include instruction in estate traditions."

"Usually, baskets of food—hams, preserves, perhaps some sweets for the children. Coal or firewood for those who need it most. Nothing elaborate, but enough to show that their lord remembers them during the season of giving." Lady Greystowe paused, studying her nephew's face. "Though organizing such distributions at short notice would be quite challenging..."

"What if we delivered the gifts personally?" Nell suggested, surprising herself with the bold offer. "Surely a few visits to express Christmas wishes would be both manageable and meaningful?"

Thomas turned to her with an expression of such gratitude that she felt heat rise in her cheeks. "Would you truly be willing to brave the cold for such a purpose? It would mean trudging through snow and visiting cottages that may be quite humble compared to what you're accustomed to."

The suggestion that she might find honest folk beneath her notice stung slightly, but Nell reminded herself that Thomas was still learning who she truly was beneath the polished exterior of her breeding.

"I think," she said carefully, "that sharing Christmas joy with those who have offered their own kindness would be an honor, not a hardship."

The warmth that flooded Thomas's expression at her words was worth any amount of cold or inconvenience she might face.

"Then we shall make it an expedition," Lady Greystowe declared with obvious satisfaction. "I'll have Mrs. Hartwell prepare appropriate baskets, and you two can serve as the estate's Christmas ambassadors. The fresh air will do you both good, and it will give the village a chance to see their new lord in person."

Within two hours, they were bundled in their warmest clothing and setting out across the snowy landscape with a small sledge bearing carefully packed baskets. Thomas had insisted on harnessing the sledge himself, claiming that military experience had taught him the value of understanding one's equipment. Nell suspected he was simply enjoying the novelty of being useful in a domestic capacity.

The village was picture-perfect in its winter dress—stone cottages with smoke rising from their chimneys, children building snowmen in tiny gardens, and the sound of laughter carrying on the crisp air. The church bells had fallen silent, but their Christmas message seemed to linger in the very atmosphere.

Their first stop was the Widow Hartley's cottage, where they were greeted with such overwhelming gratitude that Nell felt tears prick her eyes. The elderly woman insisted on offering them tea despite their protests, and her grandson, the brave soul who had made the morning delivery, regarded Thomas with something approaching worship.

"Your lordship is so good to remember us," Mrs. Hartley said, her hands shaking slightly as she accepted the basket of provisions. "We weren't sure... that is, we hoped the new Earl would be as kind as his father was, God rest his soul."

"I hope to prove worthy of that legacy," Thomas replied, and Nell heard something new in his voice—not the stiff formality of duty, but genuine warmth and a dawning sense of responsibility that went beyond mere obligation.

As they continued their rounds, visiting cottage after cottage, Nell watched Thomas interact with his tenants with growing admiration. He listened to their concerns about roof repairs needed after the storms, made careful mental notes about families that seemed to be struggling, and accepted their thanks with a humility that spoke well of his character.

More importantly, she saw how the villagers responded to him. Initial wariness gave way to cautious approval, then to genuine pleasure as they realized their new lord was neither cold nor condescending. By the time they reached the last cottage on their list, word had spread ahead of them, and they were greeted with smiles and eager welcomes.

"This is harder work than I anticipated," Thomas admitted as they made their way back toward the estate, the empty sledge much easier to pull through the snow. "Not the physical effort, but the emotional weight of their expectations."

"They don't expect perfection," Nell observed, noting how his cheeks had reddened from the cold and exercise, making him look younger and more approachable. "They simply want to know that someone cares about their welfare."

"And do I?' Thomas asked, pausing in his efforts to look at her directly. "Care about their welfare, I mean. Or am I simply playing a role I think I should fill?"

It was a searingly honest question, and Nell found herself studying his face as she considered her answer. "I think," she said slowly, "that you began this morning playing a role. But I saw how you listened to Mrs. Hartley's concerns about her roof, how you made certain young Tom had warm clothing for the walk home. That wasn't performance, Thomas. That was genuine care growing in real time."

Thomas was quiet for several minutes as they continued their journey home, the sledge runners whispering through the snow behind them. When he finally spoke, his voice carried a note of wonder that made Nell's heart skip.

"I used to think that caring too much about a place or people was a weakness," he said. "The army teaches you to be ready to move on, to not form attachments that might cloud your judgment or compromise your effectiveness."

"And now?" Nell prompted gently.

"Now I'm beginning to understand that caring might be the very thing that makes the responsibility worthwhile." Thomas stopped walking and turned to face her fully, his gray eyes serious in the winter light. "This morning, when I saw how grateful they were for simple acknowledgment, simple kindness... I realized I want to be worthy of that gratitude. I want to be the lord they deserve, not merely the heir they inherited."

The admission hung between them in the cold air, and Nell felt something shift in her understanding of what this man might become if given the chance to grow into his role with support and encouragement.

"You will be," she said simply, meaning every word.

"Will I?" Thomas asked, and there was something vulnerable in his expression that made her want to step closer, to offer comfort through more than words. "I have no experience with this sort of responsibility, Eleanor. No training in caring for people's livelihoods and happiness."

"But you have good instincts," Nell replied, "and genuine concern for others' welfare. Those are far more important than experience or training."

They had reached the rise that offered the best view of Greystowe Hall, and Thomas paused again, his gaze moving across the snow-covered estate with an expression that had transformed completely from his first assessment of the property.

"I used to see this place as a burden," he said quietly. "A collection of expenses and obligations I never asked for. But today, watching how the village looks to the estate for leadership, for stability... I'm beginning to see it as something else entirely."

"What?" Nell asked, though she thought she might already know the answer.

"A trust," Thomas replied. "Something that belongs not just to me, but to everyone whose lives are connected to this land. The tenants, the servants, the village families who have depended on Greystowe generosity for generations." He turned to look at her directly. "I can't abandon that responsibility, can I? I can't sell the estate simply because the numbers would be tidier elsewhere."

"No," Nell agreed softly. "I don't think you can."

"Which means," Thomas continued, his voice growing stronger with certainty, "that I need to stop thinking like a temporary visitor and start thinking like someone who belongs here permanently."

The word 'permanently' sent a flutter of anticipation through Nell's chest. If Thomas was committing himself to Greystowe Hall, to making it his true home rather than just an inherited obligation, what might that mean for the future? For the possibility of a future that might include her?

"That's a significant decision," she observed, trying to keep her voice steady despite the racing of her pulse.

"Yes, it is," Thomas agreed. "But not the only significant decision I find myself contemplating these days."

There was something in his tone that made Nell look at him more sharply, noting the way his gaze seemed to linger on her face with new intensity.

"Thomas," she began, but he held up a hand in a gesture that was becoming familiar.

"I know," he said quietly. "I know this is neither the time nor the place for certain conversations. But I wanted you to understand that my commitment to Greystowe Hall isn't just about the estate itself. It's about the possibility of building something here— a life, a legacy, a future that might include..." He paused, seeming to choose his words. "That might include whatever happiness fate might choose to grant."

The carefully worded statement was clearly as close to a declaration as propriety would allow, and Nell felt her heart race with the implications. Here was Thomas telling her, in the most diplomatic way possible, that his vision of the future included her—if she was willing to consider such a possibility.

"Happiness," she repeated softly, testing the word on her

tongue. It had been so long since she had dared to hope for such a thing.

"I realize I have no right to ask for your consideration of such matters," Thomas continued, his voice growing more formal as he struggled with the limitations imposed by her mourning and their brief acquaintance. "But I hoped... that is, I wanted you to know that when the time is appropriate, when you are ready to think of your future rather than your past..."

He trailed off, clearly frustrated by the constraints of propriety and circumstance, but Nell had heard enough to understand his meaning.

"When that time comes," she said gently, "I will remember this conversation. I will remember this day, and the man who chose duty and caring over convenience and profit."

Thomas's smile at her words was radiant, transforming his entire countenance with hope and gratitude.

"That's all I can ask," he said simply.

As they completed their walk back to Greystowe Hall, the house rising before them with its windows glowing warmly in the winter afternoon, Nell found herself seeing it through new eyes. Not just as a beautiful estate or a temporary refuge, but as a place where she might truly belong—not as a guest or a memory of Isabella, but as herself, creating new happiness while honoring the past.

The snow crunched beneath their feet as they approached the conservatory entrance, and Thomas paused to help her navigate a particularly deep drift. His hands at her waist were steady and warm, and when she looked up into his eyes, she saw patience and promise and the kind of quiet certainty that spoke of a man who had finally found something worth fighting for.

"Thank you," she said softly, though they both understood she meant far more than gratitude for his assistance with the snow.

"Thank you," Thomas replied, and his voice carried the same deeper meaning.

As they stepped back into the warmth of Greystowe Hall, removing their winter wrappings and stamping snow from their boots, Nell caught sight of Lady Greystowe watching them from the drawing room doorway with an expression of profound satisfaction.

"I trust your Christmas mission was successful?" the older woman inquired with perfect innocence.

"Very successful," Thomas replied, but his gaze remained on Nell as he spoke. "In more ways than one."

And as they gathered around the fire to warm themselves and share the stories of their morning adventures, Nell realized that for the first time since Isabella's death, she was truly looking forward to the future—whatever it might bring.

CHAPTER 9

A Gift of Courage

T he days between Christmas and New Year's Eve passed
in a haze of domestic contentment that Nell had never
imagined possible. The formal barriers that had defined
her first encounters with Thomas had dissolved entirely, replaced
by an easy companionship that felt both natural and precious.
They spent their mornings walking the estate grounds, their after-
noons reading by the fire in the library, and their evenings in quiet
conversation with Lady Greystowe that often stretched long past
proper bedtime hours.

Yet beneath the surface calm, Nell felt the growing weight of
an approaching decision. Her original plan had been to return to
London after Twelfth Night, to resume the life she had fled and
somehow find a way forward that honored Isabella's memory
without being consumed by it. But that plan had been made by a
different woman—one who had not yet discovered the possibility
of love growing in the most unexpected of places.

Now, as she sat in her chamber on the evening of January 5th, ostensibly packing her belongings for the journey home, she found herself paralyzed by the magnitude of choice before her. Her trunks stood open but largely empty, her clothes still hanging in the wardrobe as though refusing to cooperate with her departure plans.

A soft knock interrupted her contemplation. "Come in," she called, expecting Lady Greystowe with some final detail about tomorrow's Twelfth Night celebrations.

Instead, her maid entered with an expression of barely contained curiosity. "Begging your pardon, my lady, but there are voices in the corridor. His lordship and her ladyship, speaking quite earnestly about something."

Nell frowned. Neither Thomas nor his aunt was prone to airing matters of consequence where servants might linger. "What sort of voices?" she asked, though she immediately regretted the question. She had no business eavesdropping on private family discussions.

"Well, my lady," the maid said with the air of someone bursting to share important intelligence, "his lordship seems to be asking her ladyship's advice about matters of the heart, if you take my meaning."

Despite her better judgment, Nell felt her pulse quicken with interest. "Matters of the heart?"

"Something about whether a certain lady might ever truly care for him, and whether he should speak his feelings before it's too late." The maid's eyes sparkled with romantic excitement. "Her ladyship seems to think he's being unnecessarily cautious, if you ask me."

Before Nell could respond—or properly chastise herself for listening to servants' gossip—the voices in question grew louder, as though the speakers were approaching her door. Without quite meaning to, she found herself moving closer to listen.

"—simply cannot let her leave without knowing how I feel," Thomas was saying, his voice carrying a note of frustration she had never heard before. "But how can I burden her with my sentiments when she's still grieving, still finding her way back to life?"

"Thomas," Lady Greystowe's voice was gentle but firm, "Eleanor has been finding her way back to life these past weeks. Anyone with eyes can see that she's begun to heal, to hope again. The question is whether you're brave enough to be part of that healing."

"But what if I'm wrong about her feelings? What if I've misinterpreted kindness for something deeper?" Thomas's voice held a vulnerability that made Nell's heart clench with tenderness. "I cannot bear the thought of making her uncomfortable, of forcing her to choose between honesty and politeness when she's been nothing but gracious about my growing attachment."

Nell pressed her hand to her mouth to stifle a gasp. Growing attachment—such careful, controlled words for what she had begun to hope might be love.

"My dear boy," Lady Greystowe said with affectionate exasperation, "for a man who showed such decisiveness in military matters, you are remarkably obtuse about affairs of the heart. The girl has been watching you with the same longing you show when you look at her. She lights up when you enter a room, hangs on your every word during our conversations, and has taken to wearing Isabella's pendant as though it were a talisman."

"The pendant..." Thomas's voice softened. "I wondered about that. Whether it meant... but surely I was reading too much into..."

"You were reading exactly what any sensible person would read into it," Lady Greystowe interrupted. "Eleanor is not a frivolous girl given to dramatic gestures. If she wears Isabella's pendant daily, it's because she understands its significance—as a blessing, as a bridge between past and future."

There was a long pause, during which Nell found herself holding her breath.

"I had planned to wait," Thomas said finally. "To give her time to complete her mourning period properly, to return to London and rejoin society before making any sort of... declaration."

"And by then, she'll have convinced herself that what happened here was merely a pleasant interlude, a respite from grief rather than the beginning of genuine affection." Lady Greystowe's tone carried a note of warning. "Thomas, some opportunities come only once. Eleanor is planning to leave the day after next. If you let her go without speaking your heart, you may find that distance and time conspire to make cowards of you both."

Another pause, longer this time, filled with the weight of decision.

"What would you have me do?" Thomas asked quietly. "Ambush her with declarations on her last evening here? Press my suit when she's already committed to leaving?"

"I would have you trust in what you've both discovered here," Lady Greystowe replied firmly. "Trust that the connection between you is real and worth fighting for. Give her the choice, Thomas, but make sure she understands what choice she's making."

Their voices began to fade as they moved away down the corridor, but Nell had heard enough to set her world spinning. Thomas cared for her—truly cared, not just as Isabella's sister or a welcome guest, but as a woman he might wish to court, to marry, to build a life with.

The revelation should have filled her with joy, but instead, she found herself gripped by a terrible fear. What if Lady Greystowe was wrong about her own feelings? What if she was mistaking gratitude and the comfort of healing for something deeper? What if her feelings were real, but not strong enough for the future Thomas would need? He deserved a true partner, someone who wouldn't forever be compared to Isabella's memory.

The doubts that had been whispering at the edges of her consciousness suddenly roared to life. By the time her maid withdrew, Nell had convinced herself that leaving was not just wise but necessary—for both their sakes.

She completed her packing with grim efficiency, carefully wrapping Isabella's pendant in silk. Tomorrow, she would return it with appropriate gratitude and explanation.

But as she settled into bed, sleep proved elusive. Every time she closed her eyes, she saw Thomas's face as he had looked during their Christmas morning expedition—alive with purpose and growing affection, looking at her as though she were something precious and wonderful. She remembered the warmth in his voice when he spoke of building a future at Greystowe Hall, the careful way he had avoided pressing her for any commitment while making his own hopes quietly clear.

Was she really so lacking in courage that she would flee at the first sign of genuine connection? Was she so afraid of risking her heart that she would choose the safety of familiar loneliness over the terrifying possibility of love?

The questions tormented her through the long hours of the night, and when dawn finally broke over Greystowe Hall's snow-covered grounds, Nell rose with red-rimmed eyes and a heart heavy with indecision.

Twelfth Night was traditionally a day of celebration and gift-giving, marking the end of the Christmas season with festivity and joy. Lady Greystowe had planned a special dinner to mark the occasion, complete with the traditional Twelfth Night cake and small gifts exchanged among the household. It should have been a day of happiness and gratitude for the unexpected blessings of the season.

Instead, Nell found herself counting down the hours until her departure the following morning with a mixture of relief and devastating loss.

She made it through breakfast by focusing on Lady Greystowe's cheerful chatter about the day's planned activities. She managed the morning's walk through the estate grounds by listening to Thomas point out various improvements he was planning for the spring while carefully avoiding his increasingly concerned glances at her subdued manner.

But when they retired to the library after luncheon, and Thomas quietly suggested they might use the time to exchange their Twelfth Night gifts privately before the evening's formal celebration, Nell felt her carefully maintained composure begin to crack.

"I have something for you," she said abruptly, before he could present whatever gift he had prepared for her. Better to get this over with quickly, before her courage failed entirely.

From her reticule, she withdrew the small wrapped package she had prepared the night before. Inside was Isabella's pendant, carefully cleaned and placed in its original velvet box, along with a letter she had written and rewritten until the words were as diplomatic as she could make them.

Thomas accepted the package with obvious surprise, his brow furrowing as he recognized the shape and size of the jewelry box. When he opened it and saw the pendant nestled in its velvet bed, his face went very still.

"Eleanor," he said quietly, "why are you returning this? Aunt Margaret gave it to you. Isabella wanted you to have it."

"I cannot keep something so precious," Nell replied, hating how formal her voice sounded, how cold and distant after the warmth they had shared. "It belongs with your family, with Greystowe Hall. I have no right to it."

Thomas set the box carefully on the table beside his chair, then turned to face her fully. "What has happened?" he asked, and there was something in his voice—hurt, confusion, a dawning realization that she was pulling away—that nearly broke her resolve. "Yesterday you seemed... that is, I thought we had reached an understanding of sorts. Now you speak as though you're already gone."

"I am leaving tomorrow," Nell said, forcing herself to meet his gaze despite the pain she saw there. "I've imposed on your aunt's hospitality long enough, and it's time I returned to my proper life in London."

"Your proper life," Thomas repeated, and there was a bitter edge to his voice that she had never heard before. "Of course. How foolish of me to think that a few weeks of country isolation might compete with the attractions of society and suitable marriage prospects."

The accusation stung because it was so far from the truth, yet Nell found herself unable to correct it. How could she explain that she was leaving not because London held more appeal, but because she was terrified of the depth of feeling growing between them? How could she admit that she was running from love because she didn't trust herself to be worthy of it?

"It's not..." she began, then stopped, realizing that any explanation would require a honesty she wasn't prepared to offer. "I must go, Thomas. Surely you understand that."

"No," Thomas said, rising from his chair with the controlled precision that marked his military background. "I'm afraid I don't understand at all. What I understand is that something has changed, and you won't tell me what it is. What I understand is that you're choosing to leave rather than..." He paused, seeming to struggle with how much to say. "Rather than explore what might be possible between us."

The words hung in the library's quiet air, and Nell felt tears prick her eyes at the pain beneath his carefully controlled tone.

"Perhaps it's better this way," she said softly. "Perhaps we're both reading more into a passing Yuletide companionship than what was ever really there."

Thomas recoiled as if physically struck, and Nell hated herself for the cruelty of the words even as she spoke them.

"A pleasant holiday friendship," he repeated slowly. "Is that truly how you would characterize what we've shared these past weeks?"

Nell opened her mouth to confirm the dismissive description, to drive home the final nail in whatever fragile hope he had been nurturing. But the words wouldn't come. Looking at him—really looking at the man who had shown her such patience and growing affection, who had revealed his own vulnerabilities while respecting her grief, who had begun to build a vision of the future that included her happiness—she found she couldn't complete the lie.

"I..." she began, then stopped, her throat closing with emotion.

Thomas studied her face for a long moment, and something in his expression shifted from hurt to understanding.

"You're afraid," he said quietly, and it wasn't an accusation but a recognition. "Something has frightened you, and your instinct is to flee rather than face whatever it is."

The gentle accuracy of his observation was her undoing. Tears spilled over despite her efforts to contain them, and she found herself covering her face with her hands in mortification.

"Eleanor," Thomas said, his voice infinitely gentle as he moved closer. "Please. Tell me what troubles you. Let me help."

"You can't help," she managed through her tears. "Don't you see? This is exactly why I have to leave. I'm falling apart, becoming someone I don't recognize, feeling things I'm not sure I can trust. How can I make any decisions about the future when I don't even know who I am anymore?"

Thomas was quiet for a moment, and when she finally looked up, she found him watching her with an expression of profound tenderness.

"Perhaps," he said carefully, "the question isn't who you are, but who you're becoming. Perhaps the woman you don't recognize is simply the woman you were always meant to be, finally free to emerge."

The words hit her like a physical blow, cutting straight to the heart of her fear and confusion. Was it possible that her uncertainty wasn't a sign of weakness or confusion, but of growth? That the woman she was becoming at Greystowe Hall—warmer, braver, more open to possibility—was actually more authentic than the careful, controlled person she had been in London?

"I don't know how to be her," Nell whispered. "I don't know how to be the kind of woman who could make you happy, who could be worthy of this place, of the life you're building here."

"Then perhaps," Thomas said, kneeling beside her chair so they were at eye level, "we could learn together. Perhaps we could discover who we're meant to become side by side, without any expectations except kindness and patience and whatever affection grows between us."

His words were so gentle, so free from pressure or demands, that Nell felt something tight in her chest begin to loosen. Here was no grand declaration or overwhelming passion, but something far more precious—an offer of partnership, of mutual discovery, of love patient enough to wait for her to find her courage.

"I'm so afraid of disappointing you," she admitted, the words barely audible.

"And I'm afraid of the same thing," Thomas replied with a rueful smile. "Afraid that I'll prove inadequate to the task of being a proper earl, a worthy lord of this estate. Afraid that my feelings for you are stronger than anything I can offer in return."

The mutual confession of vulnerability shifted something fundamental between them. Here they were, two people struggling with their own sense of worthiness, each afraid of failing the other when what they both needed was simply the grace to grow into love together.

"What are you saying?" Nell asked, though her heart was already beginning to hope.

"I'm saying," Thomas replied, reaching for her hands with infinite care, "that if you're willing to take the risk of staying, of seeing what we might become together, then I'm willing to take the risk of offering you my heart and hoping it might be enough."

The words were simple, honest, and completely without artifice. No grand gestures or overwhelming passion, just the quiet offer of a man who had found something precious and was brave enough to fight for it.

Nell looked into his gray eyes and saw patience, hope, and a love steady enough to weather whatever storms their future might bring. And for the first time since arriving at Greystowe Hall, she felt truly brave enough to reach for the happiness being offered.

"Yes," she whispered, the word barely audible but carrying the weight of a lifetime's worth of courage. "Yes, I think I'm willing to take that risk."

Thomas's smile was radiant as he lifted her hands to his lips, pressing gentle kisses to her knuckles with a reverence that spoke of promises and possibilities and the kind of love that grew stronger through patience.

"Then," he said softly, "perhaps you should keep this after all."

He reached for Isabella's pendant, lifting it from its velvet nest with careful hands. "May I?"

Nell nodded, bowing her head as he fastened the chain around her neck once more. The amber felt warm against her skin, as though Isabella's blessing was settling over them both.

When she looked up, Thomas was watching her with an expression that stole her breath away—wonder and gratitude and the quiet certainty of a man who had finally found his way home.

"I suppose your aunt will be insufferably pleased with herself," Nell said, surprising them both with a watery laugh.

Thomas chuckled, the sound warm and rich in the library's

quiet. "Insufferably. She's probably listening at the door right now, ready to claim full credit for our understanding."

"As if the pendant had a mind of its own and refused to stay packed away," Nell added, touching the amber at her throat.

"Perhaps it did," Thomas said softly, his expression growing serious again. "Perhaps some things are simply meant to be."

"Merry Twelfth Night, Eleanor," he said softly.

"Merry Twelfth Night, Thomas," she replied, and meant it with her whole heart.

Outside the library windows, the first soft flakes of new snow began to fall, but neither of them noticed. They were too busy discovering that sometimes the greatest courage required was simply the willingness to stay and see what love might build from the foundations of friendship, patience, and hope.

CHAPTER 10

Twelfth Night

The thaw began the morning after Twelfth Night, arriving with the sound of dripping eaves and the subtle shift in air that speaks of winter's grip loosening. Nell woke to the unfamiliar music of melting snow and felt her heart lift with something that might have been hope—or perhaps simply the relief of a woman who had finally stopped running from her own happiness.

She dressed with particular care in a gown of deep sapphire blue—the first time since Isabella's death that she had chosen to wear anything but black or gray. The color felt foreign yet liberating, like stepping into sunlight after months of shadow. Isabella's pendant gleamed against the rich fabric, and Nell found herself smiling at her reflection with something approaching her old confidence.

The breakfast room was awash in golden morning light when she entered, and she found Thomas already there, standing by the window with a cup of coffee and an expression of quiet contentment that transformed his entire countenance. When he turned at her entrance, his smile was radiant.

"Good morning," he said, setting down his cup to move toward her. "You look..." he paused, seeming to search for words adequate to the transformation, "like sunshine after the longest winter."

The compliment brought warmth to her cheeks, but also a flutter of the old uncertainty. "I thought it was time," she said, smoothing her skirts with hands that trembled slightly. "Time to stop hiding behind my grief and see what lies beneath it."

Thomas reached for her hands, stilling their nervous movement with his steady warmth. "And what do you find there?"

Nell looked up into his gray eyes, noting how they seemed lighter this morning, touched with silver like frost in sunlight. "Someone I used to know," she said softly. "Someone I thought I had lost forever, but who was simply waiting for permission to hope again."

Before Thomas could respond, they were interrupted by the sound of Lady Greystowe's approach, her voice carrying clearly from the corridor as she spoke to Mrs. Hartwell about the day's arrangements.

"...must be quite passable by afternoon, I should think. The main roads will take longer, naturally, but the village path should be manageable for anyone foolish enough to venture out so soon..."

She appeared in the doorway, resplendent in morning dress of rich burgundy, and stopped short at the sight of them standing so close together, hands entwined, both wearing expressions of barely contained joy.

"Oh," she said, and her voice carried a satisfaction so profound it might have been audible from the next county. "Oh, my dears. I take it yesterday's conversation proved fruitful?"

Thomas cleared his throat, but his smile never wavered. "Aunt Margaret, I believe Eleanor has something to tell you."

Lady Greystowe's gaze moved between them with the keen attention of a woman who had been hoping for exactly this development. "Indeed? And what might that be?"

"I've decided to extend my visit," Nell said, surprised by how steady her voice sounded when her heart was beating like a bird in her chest. "Indefinitely, if you'll have me."

"Will I have you?" Lady Greystowe's laugh was pure delight as she moved forward to embrace them both. "My dear girl, I have been plotting for exactly this outcome since the moment you arrived. Thomas, you have finally shown some sense in matters of the heart."

"Finally," Thomas agreed with good humor, though Nell caught the slight tightening around his eyes that suggested his patience with his aunt's matchmaking had been severely tested over the past weeks.

As they settled around the breakfast table, the conversation flowed with an ease that spoke of barriers finally dissolved. Lady Greystowe regaled them with plans for the spring improvements to the estate—clearly assuming Thomas's commitment to Greystowe Hall was now permanent—while Thomas outlined his thoughts on the tenant cottages that needed repair and the agricultural improvements he hoped to implement.

Nell found herself drawn into the planning with an enthusiasm that surprised her. These were not the sort of domestic concerns that had ever engaged her attention in London, yet here, with Thomas's steady presence beside her and Lady Greystowe's encouragement, she discovered opinions and ideas she hadn't known she possessed.

"The village school could benefit from expansion," she found herself saying as they discussed the allocation of estate resources. "I noticed several children who seemed eager for learning but perhaps lack the means for proper education."

Thomas turned to her with an expression of such approval that she felt herself glowing under his regard. "You've given this considerable thought."

"I've had time to observe," Nell replied, then surprised herself by adding, "and I find I care about the outcome. These people, this place—they matter to me now in a way I never expected when I first arrived."

"Of course they do," Lady Greystowe said with satisfaction. "Love makes us larger, my dear. It expands our capacity for caring beyond ourselves."

The word 'love' hung in the morning air like a benediction, and Nell felt Thomas's hand find hers beneath the table, his fingers intertwining with hers in a gesture of solidarity and promise.

After breakfast, they walked through the estate grounds together, noting where the thaw had revealed damage from the winter storms and discussing plans for repair and improvement. The snow still lay thick in protected areas, but the main paths were beginning to clear, and there was something hopeful about the way the landscape seemed to be awakening from its winter sleep.

"I have something to show you," Thomas said when they reached the rose garden, where Isabella's carefully planned beds lay dormant beneath their protective covering. He led her to a stone bench positioned to overlook the formal plantings, brushing away the snow to reveal the carved inscription beneath: *In memory of love that blooms eternal.*

"Isabella had this placed here," Thomas explained, his voice gentle with memory. "She said every garden needed a place for quiet reflection, somewhere to remember that beauty returns even after the harshest winters."

Nell traced the carved letters with her gloved fingers, feeling the weight of connection across time. "She would be happy, I think. About us, I mean."

"I believe she would," Thomas agreed. "She wrote to me once about her hopes for this place, for the family that might grow here. She wanted Greystowe Hall to be filled with laughter and love and the sound of children playing in these gardens."

The gentle mention of children sent a flutter of awareness through Nell's chest. They were speaking of the future now, of practical possibilities rather than distant dreams. The realization was both thrilling and terrifying in its immediacy.

"Thomas," she began, then stopped, unsure how to voice the questions that were suddenly pressing at her consciousness.

"What is it?" he asked, settling beside her on the bench with the patient attention she had come to treasure.

"I need to know that this is real," she said finally. "Not just the product of winter isolation and shared grief, but something that can survive the return of ordinary life, of outside obligations and expectations."

Thomas was quiet for a moment, his gaze moving across the snow-covered gardens with the thoughtful expression she recognized as his way of organizing complex thoughts.

"Do you remember," he said finally, "what you said to me

about the difference between running toward something and running away from it?"

Nell nodded, remembering their conversation during their first walk in the snow.

"For years, I convinced myself that I was moving toward purpose, toward duty and honor and all the things a soldier should value. But I think, if I'm honest, I was running away from the possibility of caring too much, of making myself vulnerable to loss." Thomas turned to face her directly. "Being here with you has taught me the difference. This—what I feel for you, what I hope we might build together—this is running toward something. Toward love, toward home, toward the life I want rather than the life I thought I should want."

The words were simple but carried the weight of absolute conviction. Here was a man who had examined his own heart with military thoroughness and found it sound.

"I love you, Eleanor," Thomas continued, and though his voice remained steady, she could see the slight tremor in his hands that revealed the courage this declaration required. "Not because you remind me of happier times, not because you've helped me heal from old wounds, but because your courage, your kindness, your beauty—all yours alone, untouched by comparison. I love the woman you are becoming, the woman you've always been beneath the grief and doubt."

Nell felt tears prick her eyes at the simple honesty of his words. No flowery speeches or grand gestures, just the truth offered with the quiet confidence of a man who knew his own mind.

"I love you, too," she whispered, the words feeling foreign and wonderful on her tongue. "I think I began loving you the moment you steadied me in the snow and looked at me as though I were something precious rather than something broken."

Thomas's smile at her confession was radiant, transforming his entire countenance with joy and relief. "Then perhaps," he said, reaching into his coat pocket with the deliberate care of a man who had been planning this moment, "you might consider making our understanding official."

The small velvet box he withdrew was clearly antique, its surface worn smooth by generations of handling. When he opened it to reveal the ring nestled within, Nell gasped at its simple perfection—a sapphire the color of winter sky, surrounded by small diamonds that caught the morning light like captured stars.

"It belonged to my grandmother," Thomas explained, his voice slightly rough with emotion. "She was, by all accounts, a woman of strong opinions and stronger affections. I thought... I hoped you might find it suitable."

Nell looked from the ring to Thomas's face, noting the vulnerability beneath his careful composure, the way he held himself as though prepared for either acceptance or rejection with equal grace.

"Thomas Greystowe," she said, her voice growing stronger with each word, "are you asking me to marry you?"

"I am," he replied simply. "I'm asking you to be my wife, my partner, my companion in all the joys and challenges that await us. I'm asking you to help me turn Greystowe Hall into the home it was meant to be, to fill it with love and laughter and whatever happiness we can build together."

Nell felt her heart swell with such overwhelming joy that she wondered how her chest could possibly contain it. Here was everything she had never dared to hope for—love offered without reservation, partnership freely chosen, a future bright with possibility.

"Yes," she said, the word carrying the weight of absolute certainty. "Yes, Thomas. I would be honored to be your wife."

The ring slipped onto her finger as though it had been made for her, the sapphire catching the light with an inner fire that seemed to promise years of happiness ahead. When Thomas lifted her hand to his lips to press a gentle kiss above the stone, Nell felt as though her heart might actually take flight.

"There is one more thing," Thomas said, his voice taking on a note of careful formality that made her look at him with sudden concern.

"What is it?"

"I believe," he said, rising from the bench and offering his hand to help her stand, "that a proper proposal requires a kiss befitting a betrothal. And I find I am very eager to begin my education in what it means to be your betrothed."

Nell felt heat flood her cheeks at his words, but there was something in his expression—patient desire tempered with perfect respect for her comfort—that made her brave enough to step closer rather than retreat.

"I think," she said softly, "that would be most educational indeed."

Thomas's hands came up to frame her face with infinite gentleness, his thumbs brushing across her cheekbones as though she were made of precious porcelain. For a moment, they simply looked at each other, two people standing on the threshold of a new life, before he bent his head to touch his lips to hers.

The kiss defied every expectation—gentle, assured, and filled with promise. When they finally parted, both slightly breathless,

106

she found herself looking up into eyes that held wonder and gratitude and the kind of love that promised to grow stronger with each passing year.

"My betrothed," Thomas said softly, as though testing the words.

"My future husband," Nell replied, and felt her heart sing with the rightness of it.

Above them, a single snowflake drifted down from the clear sky, landing on Thomas's shoulder like a blessing. As they walked back toward Greystowe Hall hand in hand, their future stretching before them bright with possibility, Nell realized that sometimes the best gifts arrive not with fanfare and celebration, but in moments of quiet recognition—the sudden understanding that you are exactly where you belong, with exactly the person you were meant to love.

Behind them, the rose garden lay dormant beneath its blanket of snow, but already there were signs of life stirring beneath the surface. By spring, Isabella's carefully tended beds would bloom again, filling the air with fragrance and color and the promise that beauty always returns to those patient enough to tend it with love.

As they stepped through the conservatory doors and into the warmth of home, Thomas paused to brush the snowflake from his shoulder.

"Good luck?" Nell asked with a smile.

"Perfect timing," Thomas replied, pulling her close for another kiss. "Though I suspect we make our own luck from here."

And as Lady Greystowe's delighted laughter echoed from somewhere in the house—no doubt she had been watching their romantic tableau from the windows—Nell knew he was absolutely right.

The Christmas season was ending, but their story was just beginning. And like all the best love stories, it would be written not in grand gestures or dramatic declarations, but in the thousand small kindnesses, patient understandings, and quiet joys that transform a house into a home and two separate hearts into one shared life.

Outside, the snow continued to melt, making way for spring and all the new growth it would bring. Inside Greystowe Hall, love had found its way home at last.

The End

Epilogue

A FEW YEARS LATER

The first roses of the season had bloomed early.

Nell bent over a pale blush blossom near the arbor, brushing dew from its petals with a careful touch. The garden had come into full life again this spring—more vibrant, more abundant than she had ever seen it. Perhaps, she thought with quiet satisfaction, love had found its way into the soil as well.

Behind her, a small voice called out. "Mama! Look—look what I found!"

Nell turned as a pair of small boots thundered toward her. Thomas Jr.—still insisting he preferred *Tommy*—held up a lopsided posy of wildflowers in triumph, his cheeks flushed with sunshine and excitement.

"For the table," he said gravely. "Like Papa does when you look tired."

"Oh, my darling," Nell murmured, pulling him close.

From the path, Thomas approached with a walking stick in

one hand and the estate's ledgers in the other. He was trying—without much success—to review accounts while supervising their son's enthusiastic explorations.

"You've turned him into a sentimentalist," he said mildly as he leaned down to press a kiss to Nell's temple.

"I take no responsibility," she said, though her eyes shone with amusement. "He's all yours."

"Then I'll count myself lucky."

He offered her his free hand, and together they walked through the blooming garden, their son racing ahead to chase butterflies among Isabella's beloved rose beds.

Greystowe Hall stood in the distance, its windows catching the light, its chimneys trailing pale curls of smoke. From somewhere inside, Lady Greystowe's voice carried faintly on the breeze, scolding the cook for *too much nutmeg* and *not enough common sense*.

Nell paused to take it all in—the flowers, the sun, the quiet joy of belonging—and felt, again, that subtle awe that never quite faded.

Love had taken root here. And it was still growing.

The End
Did you enjoy Elenor and Thomas' story?
Please consider a review on Goodreads, Bookbub, or your favorite retailer. Reviews help me reach new readers.

Ready for more Clean Regency Romance?

The Lady Series, divided into family collections, features sassy, independant heroines and the swoon-worthy Gentle man that coax them into matromony!

Read the FREE prequel!

About the Author

Daisy Landish is a clean romance and cozy mystery author whose clean and sweet novellas have tugged at readers' heartstrings around the world. When she's not writing love stories, Daisy spends her time reading, hiking at dawn, and riding into the sunset on her horse, Rosebud.

www.daisylandishromance.com

facebook.com/daisylandishromance
x.com/daisy_landish
instagram.com/daisylandishbooks
amazon.com/author/daisylandish
bookbub.com/authors/daisy-landish
goodreads.com/Daisy_Landish

Also by Daisy Landish

Clean Regency Romance

The Lady Series - The Allington Collection

The Lady Series - The Gillingham Collection

The Lady Series - The Blackmore Collection

The Lady Series - The Norrington Collection

Clean Contemporary Romance

Timeline Retreats

Maplewood Grove Series

Love on Spruce Island

Second Chance

Cherry Tree Island

The Wedding Trio

Extra Credit

Counting on the Cowboy

Focusing on the Cowboy

Mistletoe Magic

Grounded at Christmas

Cozy Mysteries

Sophie Brooks Mysteries

Jane and Kennedy Daniels Mysteries

Pine Grove Mysteries

Annie Archer Paranormal Mysteries

Wilma Wade Holiday Mysteries

Mike and Maddie Mysteries

Mystic Moonhaven Mysteries

Sweater Weather: Cozy Mysteries for Fall

Summer Vibes: Cozy Mysteries for Summer

Let it Snow: Cozy Mysteries for Winter

Spring Break: Cozy Mysteries for Spring

www.ingramcontent.com/pod-product-compliance
Lightning Source LLC
Chambersburg PA
CBHW022037170626
46808CB00003B/1245